Advance praise for *Children of Demeter*

"Knight creates a palpable suspense throughout the deep and many-layered mystery, and her characters leap off the pages: Sara, especially, is fully fleshed out, haunted by both her past and her present. Readers of eerie horror will find much to enjoy."
—*Publishers Weekly*

"In her second novel, Knight takes on a vengeful goddess, the disappearance of a hippy commune, haunted land, and the ghosts of the past in an intoxicating tale of terror, betrayal, and rebirth. Be prepared to stay up far too late reading. I did."
—Patricia Lillie, author of *The Cuckoo Girls*

"A chilling look into cults, feminine magic and sacrifice. Fast paced with fresh ideas, Knight's tale takes the reader in unexpected and creepy directions."
—Laurel Hightower, author of *Crossroads* and *Whispers in the Dark*

"Weird, and beautiful, and scary as hell. E.V. Knight takes the reader down into a place of genuine darkness. Brava!"
—Jonathan Maberry, NY Times bestselling author of *Ink* and *V-Wars*

"I'm a sucker for stories about mysterious cults and small towns harboring dark secrets, and EV Knight raises the bar with her mesmerizing novel, Children of Demeter. This is a confident, and beautifully written, novel that sucks you in as the chilling truth behind the Demeter cult is masterfully revealed. Expect to stay up long after the lights have gone out devouring this dark mystery. That's where EV Knight wants you, and where her monsters lie in wait."
–Brian Kirk, author of *We Are Monsters* and *Will Haunt You*

Published by Raw Dog Screaming Press
Bowie, MD
All rights reserved.
First Edition

Book design: Jennifer Barnes
Cover art copyright 2021 by Lynne Hansen
LynneHansenArt.com

Printed in the United States of America
ISBN: 978-1-947879-33-1

Library of Congress Control Number:
2021937883

www.RawDogScreaming.com

CHILDREN OF DEMETER

EV Knight

RAW DOG
SCREAMING
PRESS

Acknowledgements

I must always start with my amazing husband, Matt. Without your support, love, kindness, and encouragement, I'd never finish anything.

Secondly, while this is obviously a complete work of fiction, there is, in fact, a bubbly, energetic real estate agent named Stephanie in my life who helped me immensely with this book. Characters are funny things, and have a mind of their own sometimes. I only originally meant for Stephanie to be a bit character in the beginning and named her after my friend as a thank you. In the end, I had to send a copy of the draft to her explaining that her character decided to hang out a lot longer than originally anticipated. She's super cool and didn't make me change anything. Thank you, Stephanie Jones, you rock.

My beta reader/draft editor, Virginia Nelson is a first-rate friend and best-selling romance novelist herself. She's also my cheerleader and the sweetest person in the whole world.

For Lynne Hansen, cover artist extraordinaire, for taking on my psychedelic dream cover and

Last, but never, ever least, Raw Dog Screaming Press for being the amazing publisher they are. It's personal and business with RDSP. I like working with people that I truly like. They make you feel like a member of their family and I wouldn't want this book in anyone else's hands. Thank you all so much.

For my mother, Gloria—The Demeter to my Persephone.

Prayer to Demeter

Demeter, great mother, by whose blessings we survive.

We are joyful and thankful to you, our bright and generous Goddess. We sing and dance your praises and share your bounty with the world so that they may come to know your kindness.

Grant us those things you hold most dear—make the womb of the earth fertile to the seeds within, bestow upon us a blessed harvest, and give to us too, an abundance of daughters so that we may come to understand your own suffering. Help us to accept all changes that come with the stillness of winter.

Receive our small offering, a token of remittance for all that you see fit to impart to us and for it, allow us to be renewed in the spring of our lives.

All Hail the Goddess, All Hail Demeter.

Chapter 1

The house stood in wooden rigor—flat and nondescript in every way. Desiccated vines of ancient ivy strangled the façade so only patches of pallid siding peered out over the desolate front yard. Surrounded by death—the trees, the grass—dried and yellowed from seasons untended, the dark, soulless windows reflected the emptiness Sara brought with her. She could offer only co-misery as she, too, was bereft of life. She'd come there to lie herself down among the abandoned and unkempt.

A gust of summer's wind provided a sense of animation to the otherwise morose tableau.

"It's like *American Gothic*." Sara rubbed her arms as she stared up at the foreboding architecture.

"Hmm?' The realtor asked.

"The painting, *American Gothic*, all somber and plain."

"Oh! Yes, the one with the farmer and his dowdy wife? I can see that. But, hey, it's a classic, right?"

"Daughter," Sara said dismissively as she walked toward her new home.

"What's that?"

"It's not the farmer's wife in the painting, it's his spinster daughter."

"Huh. Well, no wonder they both look so miserable!" Stephanie Pierce, the realtor assigned to show Sara the home she'd purchased sight unseen, laughed. "But you're not dowdy at all. You're just what this place needs—new blood. I gotta tell you, the whole town is buzzing for information about the woman who bought this place outright." She stopped and grinned at Sara. It wasn't a statement; it was a clever questioning technique.

Sara forced a smile. She knew by then that nothing got this woman down. Stephanie certainly loved her job and her town. Even if the sale was a done deal, she'd never let her exuberance fade.

"There's nothing to tell, really. I'm taking a sabbatical to write a book. Originally, I'd planned to travel around visiting defunct communes from the late sixties and early seventies, but when I came upon the history of this place—well, I put in for a grant, and here I am." That was all anyone needed to know, and it wasn't exactly lying. There *was* an application submitted for a grant. Andrea was all over that, but Sara wasn't going to wait any longer to get out of Ann Arbor.

Away from the University and the hospital where her failed marriage and the shocking death of her husband was suddenly everyone's favorite topic of discussion.

"…teacher then?" Stephanie cocked an eyebrow and waited.

Sara, pretending she'd paid attention to the previous half of the sentence, answered her question. "Yes. I teach—taught—sociology at the University of Michigan. I study countercultures of the United States, specifically the anti-war movement…um, hippies."

"Ah, and no doubt you've found a lot of interesting fodder on the internet about The Children of Demeter commune." Stephanie winked. "Well, I hope the place doesn't disappoint. I've been a realtor for twenty years here in West Burma, and I'll admit this place has changed hands more than a few times since the Demeter commune abandoned it. But the problem isn't ghosts or mysterious happenings, it's the soil up here. Nothing's grown since the group disappeared. Plus, honestly, it's a big house with a lot of land. I hope you've got some help coming." She'd started walking toward the house, leading Sara who followed with little interest. Stephanie paused, seeming to wait for Sara to confirm that, yes, of course her husband would be coming soon, and her sons or sons-in-law were driving the giant moving truck even as they spoke.

Instead, Sara shrugged.

"I'll be fine." Then, to keep the conversation friendly, she added, "I don't believe in ghosts or curses or any of that nonsense. Also, I'm no farmer."

Stephanie nodded. "Good. Well, then, let's show you your new place. Oh, and you have some great friends! One of them hired a cleaning crew to come up and get the place spit-spot before you got here. I know they got at least the upstairs done. They'll probably be back tomorrow for the rest. It's a big place."

Andrea—what a god-send.

Growing up in rural Mid-Michigan, Sara had been inside plenty of farmhouses, and this one in middle-of-nowhere Wisconsin was not much different than her past experiences. Inside, the heat was oppressive. Air conditioning was not a luxury most farm families felt necessary. The interior was just as she'd imagined. Large, sturdy, darkly-painted hardwood floors were covered in thin carpeting that over time pulled away from the dried glue beneath to form folds and undulations. Of course, it housed plenty of bedrooms the size of prison cells to accommodate the large family of a mid-century farmer.

There, in what Sara considered "the Demeter house," the only difference was the living room's largest wall. Beneath a layer of cheap white paint—likely applied by one of the previous owners—a faded but once brightly-colored mural seeped through. She could make out wide, sweeping arcs and curves reminiscent of the groovy, psychedelic posters and album covers from the original era of the house.

Otherwise, there was nothing special or interesting about the place. Dusty, empty rooms held their secrets as if nothing ever happened there. Stephanie proudly showed her the owner's bedroom on the first floor. Tucked into the right corner of the house, the room sat just off the foyer, which itself was little more than a few square feet of space. The bedroom featured a fire place—nothing fancy, of course, just a plain, red brick square—and one window facing the front yard. Sara knew she would not stay in that dark, claustrophobia-inducing room.

Returning to the foyer, and continuing into the living room would provide access to the kitchen a half bath and several more bedrooms beyond that.

"The upstairs has four more bedrooms, for a total of seven altogether. Only one bathroom up there, but let me show it to you. The claw-foot tub is to die for." She bounded up the narrow wooden stairway, likely assuming Sara would follow, but the open bedroom door at the top of the stairs caught Sara's eye. Light streamed through and lit it a bright white. Drawn to it, she turned away from Stephanie and to the window. Behind the house, about thirty feet away, a large, quiet lake reflected the June sky so perfectly, Sara felt disoriented by the view. If she'd jumped out the window just then, it appeared she would fall up instead of down.

Stephanie's voice interrupted her musing. "It's too bad about that lake. No one can explain it. One day there were fish and, the next day, it was sterile. Nothing."

Stephanie had found her. She sidled up to Sara at the window and pointed at the ragged dirt cliffs beyond the lake. "This entire property is in a sort of crater. When we're done here, I'll take you around the side of the house. On the far west border of the property, there's a rockier cliff with a couple caves. You can't really get to them, though because it's all swampy between the house and the cliff." She sighed. "The water is quite pretty, regardless, and it's mirror still, unless the wind blows pretty hard. Otherwise, it's protected by the cliffs."

She clapped the dust off her hands. "This would make a great writing room, wouldn't it?"

No, Sara decided. *It wouldn't*. It was going to be her bedroom.

She had a month before Andrea and the others arrived and set up camp—a month to hear the story this place had to tell about the group of people who called themselves the Children of Demeter. A people who'd peacefully cultivated the land for five years before they just seemed to disappear off the face of the earth, sending their land into mourning.

Stephanie was right when she said there were plenty of stories on the internet about the place, about the house and land being haunted, cursed, poisoned and whatnot. Maybe it had to do with soil drainage, whether due to some mineral runoff from the cliffs making the water too alkaline or acidic or something else entirely. But she'd noted the farm neighboring the land on the trip there. Strange finger-like projections of dead and dying crops seemed to be insidiously creeping into the lush green fields of corn and soybeans. Something changed after the Demeter commune left—or maybe the change caused them to leave.

Without another word, Stephanie headed back downstairs. She'd apparently given up on selling the tub to its new owner.

"Okay, are you ready to go have a look outside?"

The woman never quit. Sara guessed Stephanie was probably the same age as she, maybe a few years older—about fifty. That's where their similarities ended though. Sara was tall and thin—spindly, Phil used to say—with long, frumpy, graying blonde hair. Stephanie was plump as a peach. It looked good on her, as if her body were meant to carry that exact amount of weight. She was perfectly proportioned, her face full in a way that kept all the wrinkles at bay and left a permanent rosy shade to her cheeks. Sara envied the choppy texture of her short brown hair. In fact, she envied everything about the woman who seemed so well-suited for her body, her job, her life.

Meanwhile, Sara's prime had certainly passed.

"Actually, Stephanie, I think I can probably manage on my own from here. I really appreciate everything you've done to make this process so simple." She leaned against the baluster at the bottom of the stairs. "But it's been a long day. I didn't sleep so great in the hotel last night, and then the closing this morning, and the drive up here—I didn't realize it was so far out of town. I'm beat, and I still have to unpack."

"You're not going to sleep here tonight, are you? There's no furniture. Come on back to town with me. I'll get you set up at a great little bed and breakfast and take you to Slims for dinner, my treat."

Sara opened her mouth to argue that she'd be fine when her phone started ringing. She held a finger up to the agent. "One sec, that might be the movers asking for directions." She ran to the kitchen where she'd left the phone lying on the counter.

The caller ID displayed her mother-in-law's name. *Or is she my ex mother-in-law? My mother-in-law mortally removed? My widow-in-law?* She realized the phone still rang in her hand as she made morbid jokes in her head. It didn't matter, because she had no intention of answering. The memorial service was over, the cremains were theirs to do with whatever they wanted. They could sprinkle them over his mistress's brain-dead body in the ICU and hope for a miracle for all she cared.

She owed the woman nothing. *That's not right. She loved you in her own way. It's not her fault he was a cheating piece of shit.*

Later. The moral dilemma of continuing a relationship with her dead, philandering husband's family could be saved for another day. She hit the decline button and sent the call to voicemail.

"Sorry about that," Sara said, offering no further explanation. For once, Stephanie wasn't smiling. "Are you okay?" Sara asked.

"Oh, um, well," Stephanie stammered and pointed to the baluster Sara'd been leaning against. A rust colored smear exposed something etched into the wood similar to a grave rubbing. Sara reached out and touched it. The symbol scratched into the surface of the wood was curious, but the wet nature of the red overlying it was a more urgent concern. She stared at her crimson stained fingerprints. "I think you might have started your period," Stephanie finished.

Instinctively, Sara reached around and touched the same fingertips to her butt and ran them into the seam of her crotch. Also wet. As soon as she realized it, she could feel it—that warm, syrupy flow working its way down from her womb.

"Looks like this one surprised you. My doctor told me once that stress can change your cycles. Lucky me, I haven't had one in two years now, so I guess I'm free." Stephanie knocked on the wooden trim. "I bet I've got some tampons or at least a pad in the car, to hold you over til you can get to the store."

Sara heard the words coming out of the agent but none registered. *This is impossible. I haven't had a period since I lost the baby. They said never again. Oh God, it's cancer.* The screen door slammed shut, bringing Sara out of her panicked thoughts. Stephanie jogged to her car. Sara stared down at her fingertips, turning sticky as the blood on them dried, trying to recall what the syndrome was called. Sheeran or Sirhan syndrome? Something like that. A brain gland that shut down when she lost so much blood, when she lost the baby.

The only baby she had or would ever have.

"Got some!" Stephanie yelled holding up a bouquet of feminine products in victory. She grabbed a bag from her backseat and trotted back up to the front door. "Here," she said, handing Sara the pads and tampons. She rummaged in the bag and came up with a pair of sweatpants, a bottle of ibuprofen, and a pair of fuzzy socks. "I always keep an emergency bag in the back. I know the pants are gonna be big on you, but they're better than wet jeans. I'll take a raincheck on dinner tonight, but I wish you'd let me find you a room, especially now."

The woman was really something. If the town harbored any other real estate agents, Sara imagined they must sit around twiddling their thumbs just wishing Stephanie would take a vacation.

"Thank you, really. You've been more than kind. And I will absolutely take a raincheck. I think it's time I check out that tub upstairs and then unload my blow-up mattress."

Stephanie pulled out a card and a pen from the bag. She scribbled a name and number on the back. "Call and make an appointment tomorrow. Tell Doc I sent you. She'll get you in right away."

Sara's eyes filled up with tears, and her throat threatened to shut off the whole works if she tried to talk. Instead, she nodded.

"Yeah, I saw the look on your face. I figured we were about the same age. It's probably just stress." She grabbed Sara and gave her a hug. There'd been so many hugs at the funeral, hugs and pitiful looks, but it was the first one that actually made Sara feel better. Again, she nodded, her chin bumping against the other woman's shoulder. "You let me know what time your appointment is, and I'll meet ya there. Then we're going to Slim's. I won't take no for an answer." She let go of Sara and walked to her car.

Sara watched and waved when Stephanie honked the horn. Turning back to the blood-streaked baluster, she examined the etching. She took a picture with her phone before grabbing some essentials and heading back upstairs to the tub.

Chapter 2

A lukewarm soak was exactly what she needed. Good thing the cleaning company worked the upstairs first—*must have been a cool day, get the hot upstairs out of the way*—and Sara was thankful. She'd dragged her air mattress up before the bath, which made her extremely sweaty, but made the cool water that much sweeter. Each room contained a box with a brand-new air-conditioning unit, but she was going to need some help to install them. It was after five, though, and cooling down. They could wait. She opened a few windows upstairs and plopped down on the mattress to do some web searches on her phone.

"No service. Shit," she said to no one. It would be an issue for research, but for the moment, at least, the meaning behind the symbol on the baluster would have to wait. *And, if you're being completely honest, your plan to do some self-diagnosing via the internet was garbage. Diagnosis is better left to the professionals.*

"Yeah, yeah," she grumbled and tossed the phone on her makeshift bed.

There wasn't much in the car to haul inside, so she might as well do that before it got too dark and the mosquitoes came out. She tossed everything in the entryway and then decided to take a walk around the yard in case she came across anything she wanted to ask Stephanie about tomorrow.

On the way to the house, they'd passed a couple of old greenhouses with plenty of broken glass, partly covered in tangles of dead weeds and ivy. It was so strange to go from green fields and trees to the browns and yellows on the property. What had the hippies done before they took off? Why? Glass crunched under her feet, and the tall grasses and vines tried to trip her several times. Sara crouched down and dug her fingers into the soil. Dry, but not sandy. She smelled it. It smelled like dirt alright.

Why don't you leave the biology to Andrea?

She chuckled and brushed the dirt off her hands.

EV Knight

She wondered what sorts of plants they'd grown there. Marijuana, no doubt. It just made no sense that the Children of Demeter—who'd made their living off of the fruits of their harvest, who'd put in these greenhouses, built beehives, and planted an orchard—would poison everything when they'd left. That wasn't the norm for anti-establishment groups like theirs. Besides, Demeter was the goddess of the harvest. Sara guessed they were pagans, worshippers of nature in one of her feminine forms. That symbol carved on the stairs would probably tell her more about them.

The trees in the orchard looked like apple and maybe some pears. She wasn't sure. There weren't many leaves on them, and the few that were there looked brown and crusty. *Sad. This place was probably gorgeous in its heyday.* High sticks poked out of the ground at the far end of the orchard fencing off what would be the southeast corner of the property. The sticks were spaced apart enough that she could see barbed wire running on the far side and a cornfield. Kumpula Farms—Stephanie pointed it out on the way to the property. It was one of the farms affected by whatever had leeched into the soil at Demeter.

She walked over to the lake next. It was quite large for a private residence and completely devoid of life. The tranquility of it was unsettling. No cattails or reeds marred the surface, just a sudden change from ground to water, quiescent and midnight blue. Sara looked around for a rock, something to toss in just to make some ripples, anything to disrupt the eerie dead silence of it. The whole thing was like a monster in hibernation, waiting to be awakened so it could feed again. She found nothing on the ground. She scratched at the birthmark on the back of her left hand. The dull maroon splotch fanned out in the web of skin between her thumb and first finger. It was a nervous itch. Sometimes, when she was stressed, she'd find herself scratching it until it bled. As it was, the color was broken in a lacy network of fine scars.

Her wedding band caught the light as she moved her hand. Why was she still even wearing it? She wriggled it off and without hesitation tossed it into the lake. It hit with a plopping sound that reminded her of a fish breaching the surface to eat a flying bug. She watched the ripples of her decision spread out further and further until they reached the edge near her feet. The pattern was hypnotic and then it was broken by a pale face that bobbed up from the depths.

"Oh shit!" Sara jumped and stumbled backwards. Her heart tried to gallop on its own back to the house, but her jelly legs could do little as they struggled to keep her upright. "What the hell was that?" she asked herself in a whisper.

She creeped one step back toward the lake, willing her heart to quiet down, and leaned over the edge. There was nothing there. She leaned further and squinted in an effort to see through the water. *You're looking beyond the obvious. It was just your reflection, stupid.* Refocusing, she looked for it on the surface of the water and saw nothing but her shadow. *Trick of the light, then.* She nodded in response to her logical self. *Trick of the light. Sure.*

A pickup truck in need of some exhaust work rumbled up the dirt drive. It had a company logo on the side, but she couldn't tell what it said from so far away. If there had been any foliage on the trees, she wouldn't have seen anything at all. She headed over to the parking area. The Demeter clan must not have minded hauling everything a quarter of a mile from the house because they'd built a narrow stone arch with a short wall on either side of it between the driveway and the house. A college-aged kid in a ball cap and button-down shirt hopped out and grabbed a box off the passenger seat.

"Hey, uh, are you…" He looked down at the sheet taped to the box. "Sara Bissett?"

"Yes, I am," she answered. Closer up, she could make out the wording on his truck, *Cooper Family Market, Vicker Valley, Wi.*

"Got a grocery delivery for you. There's two boxes and a case of cola. Can I give you this one? Not too heavy."

She took it, seeing the note on the box marked, *paid in full, Andrea Wilkens.* She shook her head. *Andrea to the rescue, once again.* Sara's stomach rumbled, reminding her that it had been at least six, maybe seven, hours since she'd last eaten.

She began unpacking the boxes while the kid—Pete, his nametag said—went back for the cola. Soup required a pan, so she would need to wait for the moving truck for that. She put the box of snack crackers and a bottle of Riesling aside and dug for some deli meats and cheeses. Andrea did not disappoint.

Pete arrived with the cola, and she tipped him two bucks from her purse.

"Hey, you know anyone that would be willing to come up to help me install some air conditioners? I'd pay, of course." She smiled at him, weakly hoping he'd volunteer for the job. He looked around the house and adjusted his hat.

"Not really. Most of us have summer jobs and all, so I don't know. Sorry. Thanks for the tip." Without waiting for a reply, he turned around and left.

"Okay, then. Thanks anyway." She dropped her hands and let them smack against her legs. "I hope the rest of the town is a little more helpful than you," she mumbled, then shut and locked the front door.

She dug her earbuds out of her purse and gathered up the cheese, meat, crackers and bottle of wine in the leftover box and carried it all upstairs to her new bedroom.

At first, without any cell service, she was unsure of what to do with herself. All her research plans were on hold. She stared at the apps on her phone. With the same solitary shame as opening a porn site, she hit the photo app and scrolled up to old pictures she hadn't gotten around to deleting. Phil in a tux at the hospital's fundraising gala—where he'd gotten so drunk at the 'all you can drink' margarita bar, he'd thrown up in her brand-new Escalade. She had to clean half-digested broccoli out of her carpet at four in the morning.

Another cluster of shots featured Phil hiking in the Keweenaw Peninsula of Michigan. As she looked at them, she realized she'd taken all the pics from at least six feet behind him. *Never beside him.* In one, he held a mushroom in his hand as he pointed out some fascinating structure under the cap. Out of all the pictures she'd kept of Phil, only one included Sara. She exited the app and searched for something else. If she wasn't thinking about Phil, she worried that she might start considering the thing she'd seen in the lake.

She'd downloaded a few true crime podcasts before leaving Ann Arbor in case of no service areas, so at least she had some entertainment available. *While murder might not help you forget your cheating ex, it might take your mind off the face you saw in the water. It was a face and you know it. Not yours. Something came up from way down deep to look at you. To see who threw something into its lake.*

"Shut up," she told herself. Shoving her earbuds in deep enough to block her own thoughts, she scrolled down to a podcast about the investigation of a missing girl. The whole series was dedicated to her disappearance and promised new leads on the case. *This will for sure help calm your nerves.*

"Better than listening to the house creak all night," she told herself. She stacked a piece of pepperoni on top of a slice of cheddar and popped it into her mouth.

Chapter 3

Sara woke up to the quiet and tinny sound of voices. She jumped up and looked around, disoriented about time and place. Her foot landed on cold flesh, and she shrieked. Calming herself with a few deep breaths, she came to her senses and peeled a slice of prosciutto off her heel. The voices continued from somewhere beyond the bottom of the mattress. A quick sweep of the floor and she found the phone with earbuds still attached giving the listener updates and hot new leads on the case. She turned it off. It was 9:20—she hadn't slept that late since college.

The recently cleaned hardwood floor stuck to her feet as she padded to the bathroom. She sat down to pee and noticed the pad in her underwear was clean. Not a speck of blood. She wiped and looked at the tissue. Nothing. *Weird.* Maybe the doctor visit could wait. It was probably what Stephanie had said, stress. A lot of it, too. She decided to leave the pad on just in case and dressed in a clean pair of jeans and a terribly wrinkled Wolverines tee shirt then slipped on her flip flops. The cleaning service would be back sometime today. Until then, the floors downstairs couldn't be trusted, so it was flip flops to the rescue.

She tossed the packs of meat and cheese in a cooler vaguely less warm than the house itself. It would have to do until she got to town since the terracotta orange fridge smelled like something had died twice inside it. At least the colas would be cold and free of the aroma of mortal remains. She grabbed one out and wiped its rim on the underside of her shirt. Popping the tab and downing half a can, she noticed the cupboard door was open and all of the nonperishables she'd put away the night before were gone. The only things left in the cupboard were the canned soups.

The front door was closed and still locked. She walked around the kitchen and living room looking for signs of an intruder, but nothing obvious stood out.

"What the hell?" she asked the void.

She made another sweep of the kitchen, looking in every cupboard and the other box she'd emptied. None of her coveted cinnamon breakfast bars, no peanut butter, no honey, no granola bars. The bread and pack of bagels sat on the kitchen table looking innocent and untouched. A door tucked into the far corner of the kitchen caught her eye. *Probably goes to the root cellar. Stephanie hadn't mentioned or pointed it out, but likely that's all it is. Is it locked? Is there a way to get in from outside? What if someone is squatting here?*

She tried the knob. Locked. The keys she'd been given were modern and this knob and lock were original. Sara could picture the key in her head; a heavy thing with Tetris looking teeth and a filigreed end. She definitely did not have that. She made a mental note to ask Stephanie about it. Meanwhile, the missing food would remain a mystery.

"It's gotta be somewhere." She'd moved it or put it somewhere stupid, no doubt. In the days after Phil's death and the discovery of his affair, she'd done a lot of really thoughtless things. Milk in the pantry, and cellphone in the fridge kind of things. It'd only been six weeks since his death, and the call from Shirley on top of the bleeding and the scare at the lake—she'd probably find it in a bag in the backseat of her car or in the bathroom cupboard or somewhere else crazy.

She looked at her cellphone. Two bars. *Might be enough to listen to Shirley's voicemail.*

"But not enough to call her back. Oh well, sorry about that, *Mom*." She'd never called Phil's parents mom and dad. It didn't seem right. She had a mom and dad, and the Bissett's had never exactly seemed to want to be the parents of anyone else but Phil, their golden boy. The physician and master of all things. The cheating bastard who'd died in a car accident on his way back from a "conference" with some floosy nurse named Marie. Some floosy that, after the fact, everyone felt the need to share stories about. One that, apparently, had been flirting pretty heavily with Phil for some time—not to say he was innocent, since he clearly encouraged it. Now he was dead, and she might as well be. Last Sara had heard, Marie had been moved to a long-term care facility. She wanted to feel bad, but she didn't. She felt nothing. That woman had stolen her right to grieve the loss of her husband.

She eyed her purse. In it, she knew, was Phil's cell. Since the accident, she'd read his and Marie's conversations and viewed late-night shared photos more times than she wanted to admit. She could look at it again. *No.* She'd come there specifically to forget everything. Just like the Demeter clan, she'd come to escape the life and the person she used to be and become someone new.

"I need a hippie name." She chuckled. "Summer Moon, maybe." *More like Full Moon, 'cause you're losing your mind.*

"Ah, fuck." She hit the play button on the voicemail.

"Oh, hi, Sara. This is Shirley. I was hoping to get a forwarding address, so I can send you some of Phil's things that I know he'd want you to have. And, well, I wanted to see if you'd considered taking some of his ashes. I know everything is confusing right now, but Phil loved you and would want you to have them and—" Sara hit delete. The woman couldn't conceive of anyone not loving her son as much as she did. Sara rolled her eyes.

She checked the time on her phone and was shocked to see it was already after ten. The cleaning service should be there any moment, and the movers would be calling to give her an ETA. There were not enough bars to take a call.

A faint scratching sound followed by a dull thud came from just beneath her. Sara froze. Someone or something *was* in the house—in the basement. Holding her breath, she listened. Was that feet slapping on the dirt floor or her imagination? Did a stair board just squeak under the weight of a body? She tiptoed to the door and leaned her right ear so close it almost touched the wood and held her shallow breathing once more. Nothing. She squatted down until she could try a different sense and peeked through the keyhole.

It was dark at first, but when she closed her left eye, her right adjusted to the darkness. Pitch black became black became gray as light from some small window provided enough for Sara to make out the shadow of the stairs and the distance to the stone wall about three feet from the base of the steps. It was all she could see through the small hole. There were no further noises, either. She let her breath out and was just about to stand up when a shadow darted across the floor at the bottom of the stairs.

In full panic mode, she lost her balance and fell back on her butt. She scooted herself away from the door in a bastardized backward crabwalk. When her back hit the table leg, she used it to pull herself up. Panting, heart pounding against her sternum, she stifled the cries and whimpers trying to force themselves out of her throat. She grabbed her purse and phone and ran to the door.

Running the path from the yard to the stone arch, she forced herself not to look back. Whatever it was couldn't know that she'd seen it and therefore was definitely not coming after her.

Once inside the car with the doors locked, she caught her breath and everything in her body slowed down to routine processing speed. With her brain back on Sociology professor mode and no longer caveman running from a bear, Sara decided that there was a very good chance she did not see the shadow of someone moving in the basement but likely a squirrel or chipmunk running past the window where the light came from. It made perfect sense.

Okay, so where's the food, then?

"Well, this house has sat empty for ten years, so there are probably racoons or something in the attic, and they took the food. It makes sense they would leave the cans and take everything else. If it was a human, they'd have taken everything." *There. That was it.* Occam would be proud.

Still, she needed to run to town anyway. It was as good a time as any. The cleaning service had a key and, frankly, she didn't want to be there while they worked. It made her feel weird and lazy and obligated to make small talk. She'd drive until she had good service, then give Andrea a call, meet Stephanie for breakfast, and wait around until the movers needed her at home.

Chapter 4

"Hey girl, 'bout time you called me. I was starting to worry." Andrea never said hello. It was always *hey*.

"Oh, it's so good to hear your voice," Sara said. She'd pulled over along the road beside Kumpula farm. "I got to the house around four or so yesterday, met with the realtor, and—oh! Thank you so much for all the thinking ahead you did for me. I can't believe I thought I would just show up and drag a mattress into the middle of all that dirt."

"When was the last time you bought a house in a tax auction, huh? Plus, and no offense, but your brain hasn't exactly been running on all four cylinders lately."

"Yeah, don't I know it. Scared myself half to death a few times already. Old abandoned farmhouses are like ghost story fodder, and I fell right into that trap," Sara confessed.

"Well, you got a week, then me, Reggie, and Stu are coming. If that's still okay, that Reggie and Stu come? It's hard to tell them no when they researched the commune's history in the first place. In fact, Reg is a little pissed he can't come out now and do some filming before you move everything in."

"Shit, I forgot about his podcast." She had, too. It had been Andrea's son Reggie and his podcast partner Stu who'd done the preliminary research on the commune. They'd planned to come out and record one at Demeter. She didn't really want anyone around just yet, even though alone, she kept creeping herself out. What could she say? "The furniture will be minimal, and I promise not to unpack too much stuff. I'll put all the department's equipment in the main bedroom out of the way. Plus, the basement is locked, so that will be untouched until I can find a key." *Maybe even after that. Reg can be the first person to go explore it.* "And the grounds look spooky enough; everything is dead. There'll be lots of outdoor creepery to record."

"Yeah, he's good. He's fine. You know those guys. Reg is a big talker, and Stu, too, but if they had wanted to get out there before you, they could have. They're chickens." Andrea laughed.

It made Sara smile. "Okay, well, I just wanted to touch base with you and let you know I made it. I can't wait to catch up on work gossip when you guys get here." She was wrapping it up when she remembered to add, "Oh, also, no service at the house. We'll need to fix that. In the kitchen, I get calls and I can hear my voicemail, but I can't make any. So, if you need anything, just leave a voicemail or shoot me an email. I'll try to get to town at least once every day or two to check in."

"Glad you made it safe. And don't let the ghosts of a bunch of hippies scare you away. I'll talk to Bill about the cell service, see what he thinks. See you soon!" Andrea hung up before Sara could say goodbye.

She called Stephanie and set up a brunch meeting before putting on her blinker to get back on the road. There was nothing in the rearview mirror—*of course not, nothing back there but the Demeter House, and now it's empty again. Nothing is coming for you, and no one is following you.*

The knock on her window elicited a full-on scream, followed by heart-bounding panic when she realized a man stood next to her passenger side door. He bent over, peeking inside. She couldn't move or speak if she'd wanted to, and she wasn't sure she did. If only she could somehow magically transport herself back to Ann Arbor where she would sit in her own home and admit that coming to West Burma, Wisconsin, was the dumbest idea she'd ever had.

The man knocked again and made the old-fashioned "roll down the window" gesture. Unthinkingly, she did. He backed up a step so he could lean over and fit his head inside her car, He propped himself with one hand on the roof and the other draped over the edge of her window. White hair—thick for his age—curled out boyishly from under his well-worn blue baseball cap. His tan gave the wrinkles of his face the look of soft leather. Unattended stubble of a beard just slightly darker than his hair broke through the buttery richness of his skin. He was thin but not weak or frail—not at all. The sinew of tendon and muscle worked beneath the skin of his arm, which—if it wanted—could reach out and snatch a handful of her hair.

Clearly, the man had intention, but right then, as Sara patted her chest, trying to calm her colicky heart back to its usual undisturbed beat, he only stared at her. Blue eyes the color of a stormy ocean sky took her in. Up and down, across and diagonal, they scanned her entire body. His brow furrowed and twice he opened his mouth before snapping it shut and starting the scan once more.

Sara's fear turned to curiosity which turned to annoyance, so she raised her brows expectantly. When this only brought another guppy-like expression from him, she gave in.

"Can I help you?"

The man, likely hearing her impatience, shook away his dumb and refocused.

"You the lady that went and bought Demeter?"

Trying to lighten the tense exchange, she shrugged and held up a hand. "Guilty as charged." And then, "I'm Sara Bissett, your new neighbor." She leaned across the console and offered her hand.

He didn't take it. "Big place for one lady."

Wow. Okay, then. It's gonna be this way. No wonder they put up giant wooden stakes.

"Just looking for some peace and quiet—" *Dare I tell him?* "I'm a Sociologist, and I'm writing a book on the Demeter Clan. No better place to write it, I'd say."

His brow finally released its pressure on his eyes and bounced back up high on his forehead in surprise. "You don't want to do that. Don't go digging into the past. That old saying about sleeping dogs—it ain't 'cause they need their sleep, you know. It's 'cause they can get pretty mean if you wake 'em up."

"Have you owned this farm long?" she asked, ignoring his warning. She just might have her first eyewitness interview.

"All my life. Well, my daddy owned it 'fore me, but I took over when I turned twenty. He had a stroke, couldn't work it no more."

"Oh, well then, maybe we could talk sometime? Buy ya lunch?" She scratched at the birthmark on her left hand. Good stress or bad, it didn't matter, her habit was strong. The farmer who still hadn't told her his name leaned in. Before she realized what he'd intended, he'd reached out and grabbed her by the wrist, then pulled her marked hand up close to his face.

She pulled back and twisted. "Hey!"

He let go and backed away from the car, then stopped and bent down again so she could see his face. "You get out of here. Go back to wherever it is you came from, and you forget all about this place and that book of yours." He raised a finger at her in a punitive yet fatherly way. "You don't belong here." He shook the finger a couple more times for emphasis before he turned around and disappeared into the cornfield.

Sara rubbed his red fingerprints off her wrist before she gave in to the maddening itch of her birthmark. She scratched at it until it bled and her shaking subsided. Without a glance in the rearview, she put the car in drive, pulled back out onto the road, and sped away toward West Burma proper.

Stephanie waited in a booth at Slim's. A quintessential Midwest diner, Slim's featured a neatly arranged floorplan of counter on the left, row of booths along the windows and a few tables across the back. It made it easy to find anyone you were looking for, but Stephanie waved her in anyway.

"Wow, you don't look rested at all. You really should have let me—"

"I'm fine, really," Sara reassured her. "I just don't have any of my makeup or hair goop unpacked. Forgive me. I hope I'm not making you look bad." It was slightly passive aggressive, she knew, and not true to her personality, but after the incident at the house and then the farmer, she had no patience left for niceties.

"Oh, please. Half the time, I come to Slim's in my PJs." Stephanie laughed. "I was just thinking about your *surprise* yesterday before I left and, of course, I worry."

The bleeding. That's right. It seemed like a year ago. Had that really only happened yesterday?

"Oh, you know what? It was just that once and then nothing since. I think you're right—stress, maybe from all the lifting and packing. So, I didn't make that appointment. If it happens again, I'll go, though, I promise. Stephanie, can I ask you about my neighbor, the one from the farm you pointed out."

"Roy? You mean Roy Kumpula? He owns the farm that borders Demeter."

"Yes, that one. Is he…should I worry about him?"

"Why? Did he say something to you?"

29

"Just told me to leave, said go back to where I came from."

"Neighborly, hey? Oh, Roy's just a grumpy old man. He's been wanting to own that house and land ever since his daddy died, but his farm's never been much for income, so he can't afford it. Sour grapes is all that is."

The server came by and ended that train of thought for both of them. Sara didn't need a long look at the menu, as Slim's offered items she expected on a diner menu.

"I'll have the patty melt and a glass of sweet tea," Sara announced and handed the menu over.

"Oh no! I so wanted you to try the poutine. I love Slim's. They have a different poutine special every day, but their regular poutine is always available. The secret is—" She leaned over conspiratorially, as if it truly was a secret. "They use *fried* cheese curds." She turned to the server. "You know what, Gail? I'm gonna go ahead and get the traditional. Sara absolutely has to try it."

Gail smiled. "The only reason you aren't five-hundred pounds by now is that you only order the poutine to make your clients eat it. Seltzer, then?"

Stephanie dug in her purse and pulled out a dragonberry-flavored liquid sweetener. "You know it!"

Gail laughed and left to fill their orders with a wave.

"So…" Stephanie crossed her arms on the table and leaned in. "How was your first night?"

Oh, it was great! A creepy old man straight out of a Saturday morning cartoon is my neighbor, a humanoid creature lives in my pond out back, and something darting around my basement may or may not have stolen all my food.

"You know, that reminds me, I wanted to ask about the door in the corner of the kitchen. It's locked and—"

"There's no key. I know. I'm sorry I forgot to tell you about that. No one knows where the key is, but I can tell you it leads downstairs to the root cellar. Dirt floors, nothing exciting. The whole door will need replaced if you want access. The previous owners felt it was more important to maintain as much of the original structure as possible, so they left it."

"Hmm," Sara said and ran her hand through her hair. She wanted access, for sure. Especially if the basement had been preserved for the last forty-some years. But Stephanie's tone suggested she wanted the door left alone. *But that's not up to you, Stephanie.*

"Something to think about." Stephanie interrupted her thoughts. And then, "You need a bandage."

What?

"I'm sorry, what?"

"Your hand—there's blood smeared on it. I noticed your hair stuck to it just now." She rummaged in her purse again. A real magical English nanny, this one. "Here ya go."

Rather than handing the package to Sara, Stephanie unwrapped it and held it up for Sara to place her hand beneath. Sara obliged.

"Did you burn it or something?" Stephanie asked nodding towards the red-brown color fanned out around the bloody smear.

"Oh, no. Just a birthmark. Had it all my life. I must have brushed it against something this morning and didn't realize it."

"All's well that ends well." Stephanie stuck the bandage on Sara's skin and winked.

The food came out fast and hot. Sara tried the poutine but found the fried curds took away from the gooeyness of the dish and added the extra crunch that felt out of place. She didn't say so, though, just smiled and agreed it was an ingenious tweak. *To an already perfected meal.*

The conversation was light while they ate. For Sara, it was her first hot meal in two days. They both opted for coffee over dessert and the conversation picked up to more important things than the weather and what most of the farmers grew in the area.

"What's the WiFi situation around here? I notice there is little to no cell service at the house, so I'm going to need good internet."

"You a social media addict? Me too—totally."

"No, it's just that—" *Might as well spill the beans, 'cause she's going to find out eventually.* "Full disclosure, Stephanie. I came here on sabbatical, as I said, but also to escape life for a while. My husband was recently killed in a car accident—"

"Oh, goodness! I am so sorry," the realtor interrupted.

Sara waved her off. "His mistress was also severely injured in the accident. That's how I learned my husband was cheating on me. The thing is, I'm a professor at U of M. He was a doctor at the hospital, and his mistress is a nurse. Due to that, everyone in the university system suddenly seemed to know my business. Imagine attending your husband's funeral and knowing everyone is waiting for your reaction, not there to mourn his loss. Trust me, he might have had a lot of friends on the surface, but no one really liked him. No one except me…and apparently Marie, his mistress. Guess that was my biggest mistake."

"Wow, Sara. I have no words."

"No one does, not for a story like that, which is why I'd rather avoid talking about it as much as possible. But I used his life insurance to buy the place, so I can finally write the book I've wanted to write for so long."

"Let me guess, he never wanted you to, or he told you that you would never be able to write a successful book?" Stephanie nodded as if answering her own question.

She wasn't wrong. "Sounds like you've been there, too," Sara deflected.

"Something like that. My point is, when you're held back from your dreams or discouraged about following your destiny, it makes you all the more determined, doesn't it?"

"Yes." Sara felt her tenacity return as her fear slipped away. *Fuck Phil and his narcissistic sense of control. See where that got him?* "Yes. You're so right. Anyway, the other thing I didn't tell you about last night was the grant that we're writing is for other research projects we plan to begin at Demeter House. My friend and colleague Andrea is a botanist, and our friend Bill is a biologist. They both teach at U of M and they're bringing a small independent study group up next month to start looking for scientific explanations as to what happened there. We hope to answer questions like why did the soil turn and all the fauna die?"

"Oh," Stephanie said. For the first time, some of the baseline happiness left her face. "I'm sorry if this comes out the wrong way—because I've certainly never tried to write a book—but I would think all those people stomping around, coming in and out of the house, would be a major distraction. Also, and please, put me in my place if I'm out of line, but aren't these the same people who know about your husband and all? Aren't they the very people you're trying to escape?"

For a real estate agent, Stephanie sure knew her way around psychology. She was so right, and Sara had only recently considered those possibilities. But it was too late, of course. She couldn't deny Andrea and Bill the chance after she'd basically stole the house out from under them. It was Reggie's find, and Andrea's grant request. Sara just happened to fall into a bucket of money at the right time.

"You said it yourself—it's a big place. I think we'll be able to stay out of each other's hair most of the time."

Stephanie looked dubious. "So, we've got about a month to get you everything you need to know about the place, then?" She stood and threw twenty-five bucks on the table. "Times a-wasting. Let's give you the tour and introduce you to the right people."

Chapter 5

West Burma was small. The main road into town—named County Road CL on the map and County Road Close per the GPS AI—started just off US10. Once it wound its way into the town of West Burma, the road became Market Street. After a twenty-five mile an hour cruise down Market Street, the road eventually came to a dead end at Demeter House. West Burma's business loop featured Terry's Trophies, Holy Ghost Evangelical Church, The Tastee Cone, Slim's diner, and a hardware and drug store combo cleverly named Al's Drills and Pills on the north side of the road. The south side of town featured *The West Burma Citizen*—the local weekly newspaper that Stephanie promised to come back to at the end of the tour—Need A Lift Salon, and the town's claim to fame—Bixbey's Bingo Supply, or as their sign proudly proclaimed, "The *only* brick and mortar bingo supply store in the country!"

Just before the farm country began at the southeast edge of town, a depot-like building with a long awning sat empty. Stephanie pointed it out as the Farmer's Market. Inside, a small growers co-op sold goods year-round. Outside in the summer months, every Saturday from 11-6, crafters and farmers alike peddled their wares. To the west was a residential area where most of the locals lived, of which there were four total blocks and maybe ten to twelve homes. On the east side, beyond Market, Jake's Trusty-Wheelz used cars and junkyard, Holy Spirit's softball field (which had seen better days ten years ago), and a bright orange colored creek that Stephanie said the locals call Circus Creek because, "it looks like someone dissolved a bunch of circus peanuts in it."

Nothing about West Burma stood out or made it any different than any other small town Sara had seen, yet it had a familiarity to it. A sense, not so much of déjà vu, but that nothing felt redundant—more of a sense of place. Home. As if, as silly as it might sound, with its candy-colored creek and world-famous bingo supply store, Sara belonged there.

Even as far out as Circus Creek, she still had decent service. The cleaning company called to say they'd finished up and left the key under her front mat as instructed.

"We didn't finish cleaning the large wall in the living room, though. We started, but the paint is so thin and old, we chipped some off. I'm sure you saw there is a very...brightly colored mural underneath? We were worried, if we wiped it anymore, we'd have paint chips everywhere and have to start all over. I left the name of a wonderful painter on the table. He could come in, drape everything in plastic, sand the colors—all of them—off the wall and repaint, and he won't charge you and arm and a leg, either."

"Oh, no worries. Thanks so much." Sara ended the call and then excused herself from Stephanie a little longer in order to check on the moving company. Turned out they'd got lost on the backroads of southern Wisconsin and had a bugger of a time turning the truck around, but they felt confident they were on the right track. They claimed they'd be there by two that afternoon, and a glance at the time showed Sara it was half past noon.

"Any chance we could swing back by the newspaper office before I have to get back to meet the movers?" Sara asked Stephanie.

"Perfect timing," Stephanie sang. "We have completed the tour of the quaint and wholesome town of West Burma. We'll stop by, see if Roger's around. We went to school together. He's just the guy to help."

"So, you've lived in West Burma all your life then, too?" Sara asked.

"Guilty as charged." She pulled a U-turn in the grass beside the creek.

"So, you might have been old enough to remember when the Demeter cult left?"

"Oh, don't call them that, please? Especially if you write that book of yours. Children of Demeter was not a cult. That makes them sound crazy and dangerous. They were a loving, peaceful group who treated the land like a mother, hence their name."

"I'm sorry. You're right, my bad. But you do remember them, then?" Sara pressed on. So far, she'd met two people who were there at the time of the Demeter clan and both seemed to skirt the issue.

"I remember the farmer's markets. Their food was the best. They baked breads and made their own butter with the cream they got from Kumpula farms.

I loved market day, because all the people traded and worked together so that we could make and sell new and different foods. Market days were my favorite."

"So, your parents owned a farm then, too?"

"What? No, not mine. They didn't own anything."

"Oh. It's just that you said 'people traded so *we* could make and sell new foods'"

Stephanie shrugged. "I just meant we as in everyone. Well, here we are. Let's go see if Roger's here."

Roger wasn't in. It was his day off, so Stephanie introduced Sara to the rest of the staff. Julie McKinnon, a lovely woman with a sparkle in her blue eyes that matched her pixie cut, was introduced as Roger's wife and editor. Gaff Korpi, a short, balding man with the rose-colored cheeks of an alcoholic and the gut to prove it, was the sports guy. Betty Larson kept everyone up on current social events around town and looked as if she'd been doing that job for at least fifty years. The rest was Roger's department. He was the one with the degree, Julie told them laughing.

"But you're the editor, so you must know a thing or two as well." Sara said, coming to the woman's defense of her own belittling.

"Just a bachelor's in English. Roger went to Journalism school." *Uh huh. Well, Phil went to med school, but that didn't make him less of an ass, and I'm beginning to think Roger might be the same way. Keep Julie in her place, make sure she never thinks she might be smarter than you, is that it, Rog?*

Oh, stop it, Sara. You're projecting, as Dr. Templeton might say.

"Well, I'm sure he still couldn't do it without you. Thanks for your time. You're probably very busy." Sara shook Julie's hand.

"Nonsense! Nothing ever happens in West Burma anymore. You come on in anytime. If Roger isn't here, I'm sure I can help you find anything you need for your book."

"I already talked to Roger about it," Stephanie interjected. "He probably has some stuff pulled and set aside for her already. I can bring her back when he's in. No need to bother you, Jules."

"Oh, of course. Knowing Rog, he probably did." Julie smiled.

It was fake. Sara could see right through it. After all, she used to have that exact same smiling mask and used it frequently.

"Maybe just a cup of coffee and a chat, then?" Sara said. This time, Julie's smiled reached her eyes. Sara immediately liked the woman.

"Thursdays are my day off. We'll go to Vicker Valley. The co-op there has some of the best coffee in the county. My treat."

"Deal."

"Well, I better get you back to your car, Sara. The movers should be along, and you don't want to miss them." Stephanie nudged Sara's arm.

No, she didn't. She said her goodbyes to the staff of *The Citizen* and let Stephanie drive her back to her Jeep. Before she headed home—*home. My home*—she thought to ask Stephanie another question.

"So, Vicker Valley? How far away is it? I didn't see a grocery store on our tour, and I'm going to need some supplies."

"Thirty minutes, maybe twenty, if you're speeding. I'd be happy to take you. You can also call in an order to the Cooper Family Market, plus they deliver."

Sara held up her cell phone and wiggled it. "No service."

"You going to be home tomorrow, say around one? I can send Jeff Benson up. He sells the satellite WiFi around here."

"Stephanie," Sara said. "You're a life saver."

Chapter 6

It was dark by the time the moving truck headed back down the hill toward US 10. The package with *Sara* written in thick black ink across the top sat on the table, still unopened. She'd seen her name in that scrawl so many times over the last twenty years, there was no doubt Shirley Bissett sent it. The movers brought it, explaining that "her mother" stopped by the house when they were packing it up and asked if they would deliver it as well.

Sara let it sit. Curiosity itched at the back of her mind, but she ignored it. She unpacked pots, pans, utensils, and as many dishes as she could before the hunger pangs got the best of her. She sat at the table and stared at the box while she ate her cheese and broccoli soup.

The kitchen scissors were in the drawer. She knew right where they were.

"Ugh, Shirley. What the hell is this?" She shoved the half-eaten bowl of soup away and had the box opened before her mind even decided to go ahead and see what was inside. Some fragile thing was wrapped in a clear plastic bag, kept immobile by squares of Styrofoam flanking the top and bottom to keep it from breaking. A note, folded, sat on top of the whole thing with Sara's name once again written in her mother-in-law's cursive.

Sara—

I know right now you might not feel this was the right thing to do, but you were Phil's wife. No matter what he was going through, ultimately, I know he would have chosen to be with you. I've sent him to you, trusting that you'll keep my son close and with you at all times. It's what Phil would have wanted. Please consider it.

Love,

Mom.

The note crumpled in Sara's hand. *Mom? Really? When had she ever referred to herself as Mom or when have I ever called her that?* She already knew what was in the Styrofoam tomb, but she ripped it open and away from its cushioning. Phil's urn—black obsidian with gold trim. *I'm surprised there isn't a Rolex embedded within it.* 'Trusting that you'll keep my son close…' *What a crock of shit.*

"No, actually an urn of shit. That's what this is." Sara marched outside, letting the screen door slam against the jamb behind her. She marched to the lake, where she'd thrown her wedding band. If there had been a new moon, she might have marched right into the water, but the waning gibbous reflected off the smooth surface like a beacon.

"Whatever's down there? It can have you. I don't want you in my new life." She threw the art deco urn into the water, Phil and all. She watched it sink and stayed until the ripples smoothed to glass once more. "Define *close*, Shirley." She laughed and headed back to the house.

Her foot was on the side steps leading into the kitchen when she heard the splash.

"What the fuck?" She turned back around. The water's version of the moon was doing the hula, while the one in the sky would have no such nonsense. Clearly something—*or someone*—had breached the surface. She held her breath and willed her heart to stop pounding so hard. Surely, any footsteps would be loud and splashy, wouldn't they? But the water was silent again, holding all its secrets just beneath its surface. She shivered and hurried up the steps into the kitchen, closed both the screen and interior door, then locked it.

"I need some music." She announced and headed to the boxes stacked in the living room. Somewhere within one of them, she had a wireless speaker. Her earbuds were upstairs, but she didn't want anything sneaking up on her tonight, so that meant she needed the music outside her ear canals. She found it in the third box she went through, careful to pack the others up neatly, so that when Andrea and Reggie came, they could easily move her possessions out of his video shoot.

Once connected, she had to pick a playlist. She'd made one for every mood and every activity. She scrolled through the kayaking list and one for running. She just dumped her cheating spouse into the lake, so somehow the 'Missing You' playlist seemed hypocritical. She laughed when she came to the 'Boi Bye' mix Andrea sent her before she left. "Here's a good one for on the road," she'd texted. Andrea was much better about the slang college kids used. Sara had to look it up. She opened the list—thirty songs about being a strong, independent woman and/or getting revenge on cheating ass boyfriends. *Yep. That'll work.* She hit play.

Encouraged by the progress she'd made so far in the kitchen, Sara planned to finish its unpacking. Getting one room finished and organized seemed like a great goal to have before bed. Besides, she was halfway there already. She grabbed the empty bowl off the table and stopped. It hadn't been empty when she'd finished eating. In fact, it was half full. She'd made an entire can of soup and dumped the whole thing in the bowl so she could wash the pan while waiting for the soup to cool. She knew she had. Then, she ate about half before giving in to temptation and opening the package from Shirley. She stood there, dumbfounded, in the middle of her kitchen, and assured herself that she was not at all crazy. *There was soup in this bowl and now there isn't.*

She put it in the sink, intending to check the corner door once more, when the music abruptly changed. Beyoncé was no longer explaining to her ex that he could easily be replaced. Instead, The Beatles were going down where nothing was real and there was nothing to get hung about.

"Okay, what the actual fuck is going on here?" Her voice rose to a shrill as she spoke. She tried the knob on the corner door. Locked. She shook it and rattled it and pulled at the door. Nothing happened. She kicked it.

"I know you're down there. Open this door right now!" She waited. No one came and unlocked the door. She tried the knob again, knowing the outcome would be unchanged. The Beatles gave way to The 5th Dimension who implored her to let in the sunshine.

"No. No. There is a logical explanation for this." She tried to snatch her phone up but knocked it off the box and it tumbled to the floor. The 5th Dimension returned to its proper era and Corinne Bailey Rae suggested Sara just put some records on. "Yeah, no more phone tonight, and the records will have to wait for me to find them." She turned off the music and the speaker. Perhaps silence was golden.

Now you sound like Dick Clark trying to make witty music jokes. Just stop. This happens every time you're reminded of Phil. Think about it. You got your period when Shirley called, you threw the ring in the water and suddenly couldn't find the food you put away. You obsess over the package—you don't know how much you ate. And you know the service is so sketchy here, probably the speaker losing connection and then reconnecting to different playlist. I bet you have an oldies list on there you forgot all about.

"Only, the thing is, I started bleeding before I knew it was Shirley who called," she said to the big white wall. She could see just right of center, where the cleaning crew had started wiping. Several missing chips of white paint made the blue paint beneath seem that much brighter. She turned her phone's flashlight on and shined it at the wall. The coverup paint was thin—probably a quick and cheap fix-up just before trying to sell it.

Suddenly, Sara needed to know what the picture looked like under the veil of cheap, white paint. What she knew for certain was that psychedelic art often depicted a distorted version of reality or a hallucinogenic dream of sorts. Whatever the entire group had chosen for this wall must symbolize something of vast importance to not one, but to all of them. She suspected that it might have something to do with their worship of the goddess Demeter. There was also that symbol carved into the wood of the baluster. Sara would bet the remainder of Phil's life insurance that there were more artistic endeavors within and outside the house, too.

She scratched around the bandage covering the morning's self-harm as the idea settled into her brain and grew like Jack's magic beanstalk, quickly and thickly into an obsession. Nothing else mattered right then. Not Phil, not Shirley, or Andrea, or Stephanie. Not the thing in the lake nor the thief in the basement. The only thing that mattered was the mural on that wall.

Chapter 7

Sara woke up and slapped at the phone trying to silence the alarm. The guitar and upbeat drums pounded at her brain. Only she'd left her phone laying up on the box, and she didn't recall setting an alarm. Be that as it may, The Byrds belted out a vaguely familiar breakup song and Sara was lying on her living room floor. She stood up and stumbled with a numb hip and a leg filled with thumbtacks. The phone was blank—no alarm had been set. She turned off the speaker swearing she had already turned it off last night. Then she wobbled her way to the bathroom. It wasn't until she got to the sink to wash her hands that she looked in the mirror to see her face covered in small white flakes.

Reaching up to pick them of, her blood-caked fingernails drew her attention. How late had she been up scratching at the paint on the wall? Absentmindedly, she scratched at her birthmark. The bandage was gone and the entire thing was swollen and wet, seeping like a burn.

"Ouch!" Gingerly, she washed her hands, picking as much grime out from under her nails as she could without any soap. "I guess the bathroom is next for unloading."

There were some bandages in her purse, and her purse was in the kitchen. She dried her hands on her jeans and headed off to find some. The progress she'd made on the wall stopped her. The tiny mosaic squares of blue she'd started with had spread out into a large, flat circle. Swirls of azure were dizzying but, somehow, Sara knew it was a representation of the lake out back. Even more unsettling, was the mostly covered blob of the palest blue mixed with peach near the bottom right corner of the lake. Its curves suggested something man-like standing on or in the water.

"There is something in the lake, isn't there?" she asked the house. She scratched at her hand again before getting back to work on uncovering the mysterious creature that lived in the lake behind Demeter House. Forgetting the bandage, she worked gently at the wall, once gouging it too deep and put a semi-lunar divot down to the drywall. "Damnit," she sighed, and went back at it.

She didn't notice the music in the background. The Mamas and the Papas, The Beach Boys, The Beatles, The Byrds—all bands she would have associated with hippies and the counterculture movement of the sixties and seventies played on as she sang and swayed her hips and scratched away at the wall, then skin, and back to the wall.

It was a quarter past one in the afternoon when the knock at the door made her jump. She wove her way through the labyrinth of boxes and furniture to the front door. A man, young enough to be her son, waited on the front porch in a red and white striped collared shirt tucked into jeans. His beard was well-trimmed and cut close to his face. A good-looking man with a clipboard, the kind that opened up into a compartment for loose papers, was just the sort of man welcome in Sara's life.

"Hi," she said, immediately aware that she still wore yesterday's clothes, no make-up, with dirty and unbrushed hair and teeth.

"Hi, I'm Jeff." He held out a hand. She shook it. His palm was warm and smooth. Her nails were dirty with blood and paint again. "Stephanie sent me, said you wanted to set up satellite Wi-Fi?"

"Oh, gosh! I completely forgot. Yes. Come in, Jeff, and please accept my apologies. I've been unpacking boxes all night and morning. I must look a wreck."

"You look just fine to me," he said. His words were like a shock straight to the crotch. The tingle felt good and warm, and she giggled like an idiot. His grin slipped a bit at the strange reaction and part of her knew she was being ridiculous. But another part of her had awakened. That particular organ system had been asleep for a very long time. It was hungry and Jeff looked like breakfast.

"Come on in. We'll weave our way to the kitchen. It's the only table in the place right now." She put her hands in her back pockets, strategically lifting the tee-shirt up over the lower curvature of her buttocks, thereby allowing him to see that, even at forty-six, she was still in good shape.

"Hey, look at that." He stopped at the mural and stared at the exposed picture. "What the hell is that thing supposed to be?"

Sara sidled up to him. She'd wondered the same thing but had come to sort of adopt the idea of the merman in her lake. It no longer frightened or disgusted her as it had when she initially exposed it.

"I don't know exactly. I've been calling him a merman, although it's a lake not a sea so maybe a loch-man?" She shrugged.

The creature had a vaguely human shape, although spikey, fin-like projections ran the length of its legs, and its feet splayed out as if it had worn scuba flippers for so long that the flesh just started to swallow them up. Similar fins ran up the creature's arms, and its hands were merely mitts without distinct fingers. The head of the thing was the most disturbing. If it was human once, the eyes had migrated to the top and sides of its forehead and the nose was just gone. Its mouth gaped wide, the head and neck no longer distinct. Skin just sort of draped over it all like a layer of aspic.

"It's all quite stylized you know," Sara said, coming to the defense of the hideous thing. "Most psychedelic art was meant to disturb and was frequently done under the influence of some pretty strong mind-altering drugs. They may have been dropouts and runaways, but they weren't stupid. Not at all. There is a lot of symbolism, too. So, this mural may actually be a depiction of what they believed was killing off everything in the lake." She turned to Jeff and saw the familiar look of 'glazed-over student eyes bored by the teacher's droning.'

"So, anyway, let's go on out to the kitchen. I'm dying for a cola. Can I get you anything?"

If Jeff answered, Sara didn't hear him. She'd made it two steps into the kitchen when the urn, sitting in a puddle of drying water on the table, stole her complete attention. Dried mud splotches in a footprint pattern led from the table to the corner kitchen door. She had to suppress the urge to go try the knob again. Instead, as calmly as her nerves would allow, she opened the door to the fridge and grabbed two colas out and shut the door, hoping that the rotting stink didn't have time to escape into the air.

Wiping the rims of the cans with her tee-shirt, she sat them down on the table, neglecting to ask Jeff if he'd like a glass. He'd taken a seat in front of the urn and sat his clipboard far to his right to avoid the wet left behind by its water-logged return.

44

"Oh, gosh. I'm so sorry," Sara sputtered. She knew there was a roll of paper towels somewhere. Finally, she settled on using her palm and wiping that on her now filthy shirt.

"No worries. Seriously, moving absolutely sucks. I can't believe that you're doing this all by yourself."

The warmth in her nethers bloomed again and she felt flush. "All I need is a big strong man to take pity on me." She brushed her hair away from her eyes and then pulled it back into a ponytail, twisted until it collapsed on itself and she tucked it into a messy bun and grinned at him.

He cleared his throat and shuffled through his papers in the clipboard.

"So, as Stephanie probably told you, there isn't much around here for internet options. No cable internet, that is."

"Whatever you're selling, I'm buying," she flirted mercilessly.

"Yeah? Okay, I guess you could start filling out some of this paperwork. Maybe I can go take a look around outside to see if we're gonna need a pole or what to get you set up."

"A pole could be fun."

He froze for a moment, long enough for Sara to replay her words and behavior since he'd arrived. She felt like an idiot. What had she been thinking? "I'm so sorry." She pulled the bun out of her hair. "This big, empty house is getting to me, I think. Here I am acting like a twenty-something in a bar, for god sakes."

He laughed, clearly relieved. "Eh, you're not scaring me none. Besides, you look like you clean up all right."

The next gush between her thighs was not a sexual response, and she knew it. *Blood, it has to be.* "Oh, stop," she laughed, trying to stay directly in front of him. "Get out of here before I make you take me out to dinner." She pushed him toward the door and ushered him out.

As soon as he left, she retreated upstairs to the bathroom. Sure enough, she'd bled through her jeans again. It still flowed as she sat herself down on the toilet and felt it rush out. She cleaned up, left the crotch of her pants soaking in the sink filled with cold water, then dressed in fresh clothes. Instead of a pad, she put in a tampon from her meager but charitable supply.

Only one other shirt remained in her overnight bag, so she threw it on and slathered some deodorant in her pits for good measure. Ignoring the paperwork on the kitchen table that he'd left her, she stopped at the bottom of the stairs and examined the baluster with the blood-stained symbol. Simple lines intersected in an almost religious pattern.

She'd never seen anything like it before, yet it was almost as if its meaning lay on the tip of her tongue. She ran her finger over its lines. Her hand itched. She scratched it. The patch of raw skin spread beyond the borders of her birthmark. She had no bandages big enough to cover the wound, but that didn't matter anymore. What mattered was her sudden certainty that, somewhere beneath the vast white paint covering the psychedelic mural, she would find that particular symbol again. The more she considered it, the surer she became that there would be others as well.

And the picture would be the key to their meaning.

Working at the wall, her fingernails screeched in protest at the intense pain. Each chip of paint seemed to cut deeper into her nail bed. It wouldn't do. Not at all. She had to get something to help. But what? She pondered the problem with her throbbing hands on her hips. Jeff returned and knocked on the screen door as he let himself in.

"All done out here. I think you're going to need...Sara?" He came around the corner into the room. "So, I was saying I think you're going to need to mount the antenna on a pole attached to the roof. Those caves and cliffs are going to be difficult to get past, otherwise."

"Sure, sure. Makes sense. Whatever you think," Sara said. "Any idea how to get this top layer of paint off without affecting the paint underneath?"

"Uh, not really. Sara, should I come back another time?"

She considered it. "You know, maybe? I don't need Wi-Fi right now. I'm so swamped with the move and my research. Could you just pick whatever one will give me the fastest WiFi speed and come hook it up in a couple days?"

"Oh, sure. Totally cool with me. You wanna make an appointment or—?"

"No. Just come by whenever you're free. I'll be here. Whatever works."

"Okay, I'll maybe go ahead and leave the paperwork, then? If you can just have it filled out by say—the end of the week—I should be able to come by and set it up for you. No worries. I'll let myself out." He turned back to the kitchen before snapping around. "Oh, hey! I don't know what you're doing different from everyone else who's ever tried to live here, but kudos on getting some new growth, When I was a kid, I used to imagine what this house looked like when all the ivy on it had been green." Before she could respond, he'd shut the door.

Sara waited until she heard his truck rev up and pull onto the road before running out to the side of the house. There they were, crawling up the dried husks of their progenitors—bright green baby vines, as if the night before, she'd thrown some magic beans outside.

Chapter 8

Things at Demeter House were coming back to life. The vines, Sara's body, the thing in the lake, and perhaps the house itself. But that was ridiculous.

She needed to get a grip on reality. Sara determined that that could be obtained with a series of actions. First, she would unpack her clothes, make the bed—which currently took up the majority of floor space in the upstairs bedroom—find some towels, and take a long, hot shower. Afterward, she would drive to Vicker Valley to find an appliance store, buy a new fridge and arrange for its delivery before getting some groceries. On the way home, she'd grab some dinner. A pizza sounded heavenly.

The following day, first thing in the morning, she would call the doctor Stephanie recommended then head into West Burma for a second attempt at meeting the elusive Roger McKinnon. Secretly, she hoped he wouldn't be there again, so she could pick Julie's brain about the town and its possible role in the disappearance of the Demeter clan. While there, she could look up the symbol on the banister and maybe grab a paint scraper to gently remove the veil that, in her supposition, covered up all the answers to the mystery that was Demeter.

Time away would clear her mind and allow her to think clearly. Then, and only then, once she felt fully herself again, would she consider the thing in the lake, the footprints, and the new growth from long dead soil.

There, in the house, she felt split into two different Saras. One Sara belonged there, was somehow a part of what happened to the land and loathed to leave it. That Sara believed that the depiction of the creature in the lake was true to form. That Sara was young, horny, and fertile. The Sara who belonged to Demeter House knew that everything she wanted to know could be found within— beneath the skin of its unique birthmarked wall or deep within its womb behind a long-locked door. The other Sara was a sociologist there only to gather data and research her subjects' history—emotionless, and grounded in reality.

The shower was heavenly. Warm drops massaged away the belief in monsters and sentient houses allowing her rational brain to take rein again. She already felt more in control. A little make-up and some hairspray completed her transformation into recently-widowed-but-holding-her-own Sara Bissett.

Not wanting to chance another unwelcome malfunction leading to the decade change in her playlist, she chose a comedy station on the satellite radio in her Jeep and headed to Vicker Valley. She allowed her brain to wander as she drove, choosing not to concentrate on any particular problem back home. She thought of grocery items she'd like to have, some basic home necessities, and decided she would grab some paint swatches as well while out. It *was* her home after all. When the research was done and the kids had their independent study grades, when the grant money had been used up on equipment, in the end, Sara would still be living there for at least the remainder of the year. If she wanted, she could quit entirely and never go back to the town that knew all her secrets. Phil's life insurance would last awhile, if she was cautious. By then, perhaps the book would do well. She just needed to keep it light and entertaining while maintaining veracity.

Somewhere within the boxes marked OFFICE, a book titled *Creative Nonfiction* sat yet to be opened. Sara bought it in the hopes she would be writing the next *Helter Skelter*. The book was her retirement plan. Her permanent escape.

Most mid-size small towns had a store offering basic appliances and lawnmowers for sale, alongside a few churches, bars, and car parts shops. It was something Sara always noticed. Vicker Valley had a mo-and-pop appliance center that used to be a brand name shop, based on the faded sign that had been painted over. She had a refrigerator picked, paid for, and delivery time scheduled within thirty minutes of walking through the front door—another perk of small town living, from her perspective. In a suburban plaza store, she'd still be searching for a salesperson.

The food co-op could have been a city offering. The massive interior filled with all-natural or gluten-free options intimidated Sara. Ann Arbor had its share of health food shops and groceries and this one would have been competitive in that market. The cheese selection alone was dizzying.

"Sara?"

Sara jumped. She wasn't exactly expecting to be recognized. Once she turned around, she immediately found the familiar face—Julie McKinnon, from the newspaper.

"Oh! Hey Julie, I didn't think I'd see you here today. I thought you said Thursdays?" *A magnificent tidbit to remember from that conversation and offer as a way to prove you were interested. You still got it, Sara.*

"Ha ha, yep! Wouldn't it be great if I only had to come to the grocery store one day a week? No, Rog ran out of coffee at the office, and I've spoiled him with this organic free trade stuff. He refuses to drink anything else, so here I am. Figured I'd treat him to a couple steaks for dinner, too. Wednesday's just as good as Saturday for a steak, right?"

Whatever that means. She'd said it as if everyone knew Saturdays were steak days. Roger was becoming less and less attractive as Sara's point man for research. *As if you know it's Roger's declaration that Saturday is steak day? Then again, maybe Julie's the control freak.*

"Buy ya a cup?" Julie said

"What?"

"I said they have a little café here. If you haven't got anything that needs immediate refrigeration, I'll buy you a cup."

Sara looked at her embarrassing collection. Flatbread crackers, stone ground mustard, and two bottles of wine. The cheese had inspired her. "Nothing that can't be put on hold. I'll take you up on that offer."

Cups in hand and carts parked within their line of sight, they sipped their coffee and made the usual entry-level small talk, including Julie's overbearing concern for the bandaged wound on Sara's hand. "That house is so old and dirty; be careful it doesn't get infected!" Breaking through the awkward chitchat, Julie asked the first meaningful question.

"So, what made you want to write a book about Demeter House?"

"Long story short, I teach sociology at the University of Michigan. My own particular field of study is countercultures and, specifically, those of the United States."

Julie showed no sign of understanding.

"Hippies. Hippie communes, specifically. I'm fascinated by their politics within the clan, their division of duties. We hear so much about religious cults and the sexual abuse within them. We've been saturated with stories like the Manson Family, but what made these 'societies' so different?"

"Well, Demeter was *quite* different, from what I understand."

"Yes, absolutely. My field of study is counterculture, so originally, my plan was to travel around the country and spotlight five to ten communes. I wanted to really dive in to the differences between them and cults like Jonestown or Children of God, to find out how they made their own socialism and sexual mores." She leaned forward conspiratorially. "What I'm saying is, I really had no idea how I was going to organize the book. I just like research, and wanted to write something."

"Oh," Julie said.

"See, but then my friend Andrea—her son Reggie does a podcast called *The Mysterious Creepcast*. They actually go to abandoned places with sordid pasts or mysterious happenings and do their podcast on site. They're quite entertaining. They stumbled across the Demeter commune and this whole disappearance and dead land mystery. For the past six months, they've been trying to get permission to do a podcast here. Andrea is a biology professor—botany, plants—and she'd been looking for an idea for an independent study class. She and another professor, who studies more straight up biology, got together and wrote a grant to buy the place and offer classes there trying to determine what happened to make the land so barren."

Julie nodded and appeared to be making a real effort to understand.

"I'm not really making this story short, am I?" Sara laughed.

"No, no, it's fascinating, though. I had no idea the town would be hosting a whole college class. That's great to hear."

"It will only be about four to six students. Independent study is—well, individualized. The thing is, my husband was killed in an accident and—"

"Oh, God. I'm so sorry, Sara."

Sara waved away the pity. "He was cheating on me literally at the time of the accident. I'm working through it. I just wanted to get away, so when Andrea told me about this project and the grant and the history, I knew I had my book idea. I was drawn to the story, as if I had maybe heard it before. So, I killed two birds with one stone. I bought the place with some of the life insurance money, and took a sabbatical from work for a year. Now, my friend Andrea can use her grant money for equipment and it will last a lot longer. It worked out for both of us. The class will start next month and be here for three months. Then, I'll be alone again. I figure, while they're here doing their research, I'll do all mine, so when they leave, all I have to do is hole up inside the place over the winter and write."

"Like in *The Shining,*" Julie said.

"I'm sorry, what?"

"Oh, you know, like that movie with Jack Nicholson. About the writer who takes a job as the caretaker at a big hotel over the winter. He says he'll be able to write his book, but then he goes crazy and tries to kill his family."

"Oh. Yeah, that's right. But let's hope I manage to keep my sanity."

"I don't know how you could. That place gives me the creeps. Everyone says it's cursed or something."

"Why do they say it's cursed?" Sara wished she'd brought a notebook. "Oh, wait. Would you mind if I recorded this part? I'd like to hear what you have to say, but there might be something for the book, too. I'd hate to forget it."

"I don't really know much, to be honest. I'm not from here. I met Rog in college, and we moved after graduation. Everything was already dead when we came. I didn't see anything firsthand." As she spoke, Sara dug her phone from her purse and set the record button.

"May I?" she asked. Julie shrugged. Sara activated it and saw the number ticker start.

"What I know, I've heard secondhand. Roger says it's all a bunch of nonsense. He says the hippies poisoned everything when they left, wrecked their own place, and disappeared in the night like a bunch of gypsies."

Sara cringed at the derogatory term for the Romani people. "But why would they do that? From what I understand, they had a good relationship with the town."

"That's the thing. No one knows why. I've heard there were a few complaints filed with CPS for possible child abuse and neglect, but I don't think they ever had any of their kids taken away."

It wasn't an uncommon thing for hippies. Their parents or those of that generation would often file complaints against the free-spirited way they chose to raise their children.

"I suppose maybe there was something legitimately wrong going on, and if they got word of a possible valid complaint, they might take off before anyone could remove the children. But one complaint or two is not a whole town, and it is certainly not the land they'd so carefully cultivated. Why poison it?"

"That's what I say!" Julie agreed. "I tell Roger all the time, that's the part that doesn't make sense. Demeter is like the goddess of harvest. They based their whole society around her. Whatever they were doing worked. You should see some of the pictures of their stand at the market. Their farming skills were top notch. And they had bees, and they made honey mead and jams. I mean, why would they hurt the land they loved so much?"

"Pictures? Where can I find these pictures?" Sara asked.

"Oh, we have a whole shelf in storage of pictures from all the old editions. I organized them, so I've seen every single one we have. You can come take a look. We have quite a few of the commune."

"That would be so great, Julie. When would be a good time?"

"Any day but Thursday." She winked. "Like I said, it's my day off. Roger has no idea how the filing system works. I swear the whole newspaper would shut down if anything happened to me." Her phone jangled, and she looked down. "Speak of the devil."

Sara hit the pause button and waited while Julie made excuses for why she wasn't back yet with the coffee then promised that she was currently in line and would be back as soon as possible.

"Someone is very grumpy without his coffee." She gave Sara a halfhearted grin. "Stop by any time, really. I know just where to look for them."

"Thanks so much, Julie, for the coffee and the help. I needed a jumping off point. The pictures will be a good place to start."

Chapter 9

The biopsy of her uterine lining was not as painful as she'd expected it to be. Perhaps her nerves were just overwhelmed with the shock of getting the appointment immediately after she'd called—thanks again to Stephanie—coupled with Dr. Palmer explaining that any bleeding after menopause was considered abnormal and could be cancer.

"But I don't think I'm menopausal. I just quit having periods after the miscarriage, and the doctors said I would never be able to get pregnant again," she'd explained.

"That's why we're going to run some labs as well. I'm not sure why they felt so certain that you'd never get a period again or be able to conceive. There are some rare conditions, like Sheehan's syndrome, that can cause that, but from what you've described, it doesn't line up. Don't worry. We'll get to the bottom of it."

Dr. Palmer's assurance was comforting, but it wouldn't do anything for her until she got the results back at her follow up appointment in two weeks. Until then, she'd need distraction.

On the way home, she stopped at Drills and Pills, still shaking her head at the absurdity of the name. With a paint scraper in hand, Sara stood in front of the vast array of paint chips in colors with names like "Scottish Field" and "Baby's Blush." No single color stood out as THE ONE for her bedroom or her study. She plucked a shade she liked from every hue offered and shoved them in her purse. Perhaps in the light of Demeter House, one would declare itself.

"Can I help you with anything?" an elderly gentleman wearing the tell-tale red vest of an employee asked.

"Oh, no." Sara sighed. "Just getting lost in all the color options."

"Thinking of painting a room?"

"Don't know, maybe the whole house. I just bought it and every room is white."

"Ah. You must be the young lady that bought the old Schmidt house up on the hill."

"Uh...I'm not—"

"The hippie house. Used to be owned by Schmidts. Nice German couple built it, then one of their grandsons turned it into the commune. Guess I'll always think of it as the Schmidt place."

"Oh, wow. Okay. Yes, I'm Sara Bissett." She put her hand out, and he took it. His hearty palms were warm and enveloped hers. "I didn't know about the Schmidts. I'm writing a book on the history of the place."

"So I've heard. Yes. Got a whole slew of college people coming up as well. Stephanie told us."

Does anyone in this town not know Stephanie?

"You know Stephanie?" she asked. It was rhetorical, of course. Clearly, he did. She just had nothing else to offer. One would think the whole town was trying to keep a secret. No one seemed happy about a group of individuals coming from the University.

"I should hope so. She's my granddaughter." He grinned and then seemed to remember he hadn't given her his name. "Walt Pierce."

"Sara Bissett, so nice to meet you. Stephanie's a life saver, really. You must be proud." "Yes ma'am. Raised her since she was eight or ten. Round then, anyway."

"Oh!" She hadn't expected that.

"Well, I guess, if you want my advice, and I know you didn't ask for it, but if you do, I'd tell ya not to go fishing around too much up there. The place ain't right anymore. Those hippies did something before they all drank the Kool-Aid and disappeared."

"Drank the Kool-Aid? Are you saying they committed mass suicide?" This was the first she'd heard that theory.

"Eh, just my opinion. Not suicide exactly, but something like it. Anyway, point is, no one stays there for long. I wouldn't go putting much effort into painting the place."

"Huh. Well, thanks for the advice. Any chance you might be willing to let me interview you for my book one of these days?" Sara ventured.

"Told ya all I know, but I'm here most days. If you want to come by and put it on paper, I don't see the harm." He smiled. "Now, is there anything else I can do for you?"

"Do you know how to open a locked door without a key?"

"'Zat some kinda riddle?" He laughed.

"No, unfortunately not. The basement door up at the house is locked, and Stephanie doesn't have the key. I'd hate to damage the door. It's original."

"Nothing in that basement but an old root cellar. Dirt floors, old stone walls, and a lot of mold. Better off with it locked. You don't want critters comin' in."

But they already have. That's the thing—they're already in.

"Hmm. Well, then." She held up the paint scraper. "I guess I'm ready to check out."

Her new ritual, after arriving back at Demeter House, involved checking cupboards for missing food, wriggling the knob on the basement door, and searching for footprints or signs of recent intrusion. She found nothing new to report. Phil's urn sat dry on the table where she'd found it. For a moment, she considered the idea that she had never thrown it in the lake at all. But that wasn't true. She *had* thrown it out.

"Because I can't stand having you here. I left you behind, Phil. I left you in Ann Arbor with your stupid whore." She touched the urn, ran her finger down the side of it, then shoved it further from the center of the table. "How could you? I know things weren't great, but I loved you. I gave up so much for you. You could have told me you weren't happy. You should have said something."

The tears hung on the rim of her eyelids, and she wasn't going to try to hold them back anymore. There was no one here to see. No one to judge her. She let herself collapse to the floor and cry. She curled up in a fetal position and ugly cried until her stomach hurt, her face ached, and her cheek was soaked from the tears mixed in a puddle of drool that spilled from her contorted mouth.

When silence overtook her and the sobs subsided, she heard scratching. No, more like a pawing sound on the far side of the basement door. Without getting up, she crawled on hands and knees over to it and tried to peek underneath. She saw nothing but darkness. She scratched against her side of the wood. Whatever it was responded with a mimicked reply. She repeated the scratch in a different rhythm; it echoed back the same.

"Hello?" she whispered to the door. "Is someone there?"

No response. She tried looking through the keyhole. *Too dark.*

"I won't hurt you," she said, and leaned her body against the door. Pawing at it with her right hand, then stroking the door, she said, "I don't want to be alone here tonight. If there is someone there, can you say so?"

Silence.

"Why'd he have to cheat on me? Why'd he have to go and do that and then die? I'll never know. Never." She outlined the lock panel with her finger. "I tried to be a good wife. Goddamnit! My husband's dead, and I don't know what I'm supposed to feel! Just say something! Tell me what I'm supposed to feel?"

There was a hiss or sigh from the other side of the door, and Sara gasped. She held her breath and listened, ear pressed to the keyhole. Something breathed. She was sure of it. Her heart stomped up the steps of her throat and into her ears until she couldn't hear anything but its frightened pacing.

Slowly and as silently as she could, she pulled her phone from the pocket of her jeans and turned on the flashlight app. She brought her eye to the keyhole again and angled to light so she could see.

It was just a flash, no more than a fraction of a second, but Sara saw it. An eye, the same color gray as hers, stared back through the hole. Then it blinked and was gone. Sara stood up and knocked hard on the door.

"Hey! Hey! I saw you. I saw you in there. Come out here right now. Who are you?" She leaned her head against the door.

Silence. Nothing. No movement, no breathing. No scraping or pawing against the door. Her hand itched madly. She scratched at the healthy skin around the healing crater and managed to widen the diameter of the wound by a few millimeters. She waited for what seemed like hours for any sign to corroborate what she'd just seen—something to prove there was another being on the other side of the door. Whatever it was must have somehow vanished, though, because even after her heart descended into its rightful place in her chest, the house was void of sound.

There had to be a way into the basement from outside. She decided that, even if there wasn't, outside seemed like a good place to be just then. Besides the lake and a quick look near the greenhouses, she hadn't really taken a good tour of the grounds. A lovely summer day shouldn't be spent unpacking boxes that could easily wait. A haunted house needed to be accepted in small sips, not giant gulps. She'd had a taste of it for now. Later, after a couple glasses of wine, she'd spend a longer bit of time.

Chapter 10

Sara carried a bucket out to the greenhouses and threw in any large chunks of glass she could find. She cursed herself for not getting a pair of work gloves while she was out, but she knew there was a pair somewhere still packed away. It wasn't like she was in serious cleanup mode, anyway. She picked at any pieces she kicked into with her feet, but mostly she was just out to see if anything had started to grow. Some tiny little mushrooms pushed through the surface in a few areas once flattened by chunks of glass, but it was new growth, and that meant something had changed.

Bent over examining the shoots, she felt as if someone was behind her. Hairs on the back of Sara's neck erupted in a mimicry of the small growth she inspected. Had the ghost from the basement followed her out of the house? She stood up and twisted around. Behind her and to the left, Roy Kumpula watched from his field. He appeared to have been collecting a sample of his crop.

Sara stared him down, daring him to just try to frighten her again. He said nothing and went back to his work. Ignoring the continued feel of surveillance, Sara walked the perimeter of the border between Demeter house and Kumpula farm. There, at the base of each wooden stake, small green vines coiled out of the ground straining towards the stability of the wooden pole so they could start their climb.

Good. I hope they grow fast. No wonder the hippies put these poles up. I bet they all got tired of Roy gawking at them every time they went outside.

As she headed past the front of the house and around to the far side, she stole a glance into the field. Roy hadn't moved at all since she'd last looked. He was watching her, no doubt. She tried her best to ignore him.

She hadn't really taken a good look at that side of the house. Stephanie had mentioned that most of the land on that side was swampy, but the swamp didn't start until well past the lake's border. That being said, there wasn't much to be seen in the yard except a round, flat cement slab that lay, unassuming, among the brown scrub grass. Sara suspected it was the lid to a well.

She bent down to wipe the dead grass and debris off before trying to move it. In the center, carved into the cement itself, was the same symbol as on the baluster. Sara traced it with her finger. There was a power there, something ancient and deep.

Suddenly, a thought came to her. What if it wasn't a well at all? What if, beneath the cover, there was a ladder, and that ladder led to a tunnel which led to the basement of the house? *How silly. How utterly insane. The thoughts of a lonely, paranoid woman.* Yet…what if? There had certainly been enough unusual things going on around there to warrant crazy ideas like that. She checked on her stalker once more. Roy no longer even tried to pretend he wasn't spying on her. He stared silently, hands at his sides like some 80's slasher flick serial killer. She shivered away goosebumps and crouched to her knees.

She pushed with both hands, but the lid didn't budge. She dug her feet into the ground and got into a downward dog position. Using her legs as well as her upper body, she tried again—no movement. Lastly, she sat on her butt and pushed at the cement with her feet.

"No reason for you to be moving that cover," Roy called. He'd crept closer—almost trespassing onto *her* land. She twisted her torso toward him.

"I'm not sure it's any of your business," Sara called back. He was still far enough away that he probably couldn't see her shaking. "I'd appreciate it if you'd just keep to yourself. No reason for you to be out here monitoring everything I do."

"There is, actually," he argued. "You're in danger here, and you can't seem to stop making it worse for yourself."

"You know, this isn't some Lifetime movie, and you don't need to talk like some mysterious villain. If you have something to say, you should say it." She approached him. *Enough of this. He is an old man, what's the worst he could do?*

He is a fit, healthy old man who farms every day. I bet he could hurt *you, if he really wanted to.*

Maybe, but if he wanted to, he would have by now.

Three feet, at most, separated them.

"Look, I don't mean to frighten you—"

"Well, you're doing just that," she interrupted.

His eyes met hers for what seemed like five minutes, then he turned around and walked into his crops.

"What the fuck is wrong with people around here?" she yelled. Roy didn't stop, just kept walking as if she'd said nothing.

Sara'd had enough. When Reggie and Stu came with Andrea, they'd help her move this slab. Right then, she was hungry and thirsty, and the very real person outside was scarier than the perceived one behind her basement door.

The house was hot. Stifling. Those air conditioners weren't going in until Reg and Stu arrived. She opened every window in the place, starting in the kitchen. Just before heading into the living room, she tried the corner door again. Still locked.

"You're psycho. Clearly not doing well alone," she announced to herself. "Get a grip, Sara."

The lunch plate of cheese and crackers went fast. She considered another helping when the urn sitting on the far side of the table, where she'd pushed it away earlier, caught her attention—black and sleek with its haughty gold trim. She grabbed a knife out of the drawer and scooped up the remains of her husband. Sitting on the floor, in front of the baluster, she scratched a copy of the symbol onto the surface of the urn. The double X was perfect and easy enough, but the semicircle at the top looked more like a V using such a crude instrument. But she thought whatever supernatural meaning it had would come through anyway.

"It's the thought that counts, right, Phil? You weren't thinking of me at all, so this is more than you deserve."

Now that the perfect surface was marred, she felt a little better. She wasn't sure what she had intended on doing with it once her little craft project was done.

You know exactly what you're going to do with it. You're going to get the guys to move that lid then you're going to toss it down into the earth.

That was exactly what she wanted to do, yes. But would her friends object? Tell her she was being rash, to give it some time. Put the urn in the back of the closet for now. Out of sight and all. Or would Andrea celebrate the idea? She wasn't sure. For the moment, it could stay on the floor by the stairs. She'd figure it all out later.

The well, or whatever lay beneath that stone, intrigued her. Why did they carve the symbol into it? What was so important about it? She had an idea. If it was that important, the reason could be found in the mural on the wall. Had they painted the well into the picture? Her hand itched as a proxy for the wall. "Come," it said. "Come reveal the mysteries."

The boxes piled up waiting to be unpacked in the August heat—didn't matter like that mural. The answers were there. She knew they were.

Chapter 11

She'd uncovered a somewhat warped depiction of the house and a new symbol at the webbed feet of the lake monster. This one looked like two sideways lightning bolts held up on two fenceposts. Swirls of green filled the space between house and lake. Verdant vines with tiny white, yellow, and blue flowers climbed the sides of the house, softening its corners and giving a roundedness to the roof.

Her arm ached with the repetitive motion of the scraper and her hand itched as if it too held secrets beneath her flesh. The air had cooled considerably with nightfall, and turned her beads of sweat into snowflakes. She shivered and her stomach rumbled. Sara hadn't eaten or drank anything since her lunch of cheese, crackers, and a single can of cola she'd opened when she'd first come in. There was a swallow left, but it was warm and flat.

No sounds emanated from the cellar door since her attempt to move the cement slab. She'd purposefully left the music off in case her basement dweller returned. Plus, if Roy Kumpula started snooping around the property, she wanted to hear him, too.

The doorbell rang just as Sara decided to get something to eat. Before she reached the foyer, the front door creaked open. Stephanie poked her head in and yelled, "Hello? Sara?"

"Coming," she called jogging to where Stephanie now stood inside the entryway. She wanted to be irritated, but when she saw the bag in the woman's arm and smelled food, her stomach lurched in desire, Sara forgot her irritation.

"I thought you could use a little pick-me-up. Something tells me you're the type to work right through lunch and dinner. You need to eat."

"Stephanie, I think I love you! Come on in." She saw the flick of the woman's eyes down to the scratched-up urn on the floor and was grateful when her new friend said nothing.

As they maneuvered through a small path between stacks of boxes in the living room, Stephanie stopped at the mural.

"So, you're taking the paint off this mural instead of covering it?" It didn't feel like a judgement, just a question. Sara appreciated that.

"Yeah, I mean, I was curious, but then when I came across this guy here…" Sara pointed to the lake monster. "I had to know what the whole thing looked like."

Stephanie reached up and touched the creature. She slid her finger across it as if reading braille.

"Let's get this bag off your hands," Sara said when Stephanie's reaction grew uncomfortable.

"Oh, yeah of course. So, what do you think of that?" She followed Sara into the kitchen.

"I'm guessing the landscape part was painted first and the monster added later." Sara unpacked the brown paper bag. The smell of fried food and beef gravy almost made her heave with hunger.

"How could you know that?" Stephanie rummaged through a purse roughly the size of a small suitcase.

"Because the landscape is done in one style, very reminiscent of its time. But the monster is different, more like the artist was trying to give a true depiction. My guess is it was seen during a bad trip and added as a means to recall it later."

"Makes sense." Stephanie pulled two unlabeled bottles out of her purse. "Mead, made by The Children of Demeter clan. Purchased by my grandparents and saved in their wine cellar all this time. One for you to keep and one for us to enjoy." She grinned.

"My God, Stephanie!" Sara grabbed a bottle. "Are you serious? This is amazing. We can't get any closer to them than this."

"Not anymore," Stephanie agreed.

Sara poured while Stephanie divvied up their dinners which consisted of French dip sandwiches, onion rings and small fried but unbreaded cheese cubes that Stephanie insisted were a regional specialty.

Stephanie quieted as she ate and Sara scarfed her meal, enjoying the cheese more than her waistline would have liked.

"So, you had to have been what, five or so when the clan disappeared?" Sara asked after they'd slowed down to picking at crumbs and breading from the onion ring box. She was on her second glass of the spicy-sweet mead and feeling the buzz.

"I was eight, actually. What? Don't look at me so shocked like that. I look young for my age."

"Do you remember seeing them around town and whatnot? Clearly your grandparents went to the farmer's market." Sara shook her glass. Stephanie laughed and emptied the bottle into her glass. She'd not even finished her first and Sara was now onto her third and final one.

"Sure. They were good people, Sara. Never caused any problems. Some people didn't like them because they were hippies or because they let their kids run around naked in the summer. Some because they worshipped the earth goddess and not the god of most religions."

"So, they really worshipped Demeter? It wasn't just a hippie kind of name?"

"What's wrong with worshiping Mother Earth? Is it any sillier than worshiping an invisible man in the sky?"

"No. No. Of course not." Sara held her hands up in surrender. She sipped her mead and found within the glass her courage to ask more questions. "What does it mean, *they worshipped Mother Earth*? Were there special rituals or offerings?"

"Don't all religions have rituals?"

"Touché," Sara said.

"Here's the thing, Sara. You're going to hear all kinds of rumors and nonsense about The Children of Demeter. I was just a kid, but all I ever saw was a group of loving, peaceful individuals who took care of the land the best they could. They worked and they devoted themselves to their Goddess and then they were betrayed." She stopped abruptly. "I don't know, I was just a kid."

"Betrayed by whom?" Sara prodded.

"It's a theory I have. That's all. No need to add to the rumors I warned you about."

"Come on, Stephanie," drunk Sara pleaded. "Don't dangle all that drama in front of me. What do you think happened to them?"

"They disappeared, and I'm not sure they're ever coming back." She got up and rinsed her glass out in the sink. "Now it's your turn, Sara. Tell me about your childhood. Where were you born?"

"I don't know. I was left on a bench at a mall when I was probably only a few days old. A young couple found me and took me to the hospital. Relatives of the couple took me in for foster care for about a month then adopted me. I assume I was born in Ann Arbor or very near at least. My parents were both professors at the university. I grew up an only child and they loved me like their own, so I've never felt like I was missing anything."

"Oh wow. I'm so sorry to have brought that up." She brushed at her hands. "Must be the mead loosening my lips. Probably better head out before I talk you into opening that second bottle."

"No rush, really." Sara was about to offer the second bottle in the hopes that Stephanie would talk more about the clan, but suddenly their visit was over.

"I'm going to find a couple guys to head up here and help you get those air conditioners in before your friends get here. And, if you need some help unpacking, I have Saturday free."

Always so helpful. *Except when it comes to information on the clan. Then she isn't so forthcoming.* She supposed most people in the town had theories and strong feelings about The Children of Demeter. She just needed to find someone willing to share them.

"That'd be so great, Stephanie. I'll buy lunch next time."

"Can I give you a friendly piece of advice?" Stephanie asked, standing at the front door.

"Of course."

"I'd leave the mural alone for now. Get these boxes unpacked and put away. Wouldn't want your friends thinking you've lost it up here all by yourself. They might never leave."

Chapter 12

Sara took Stephanie's advice. For the next three days, she ignored the mural, bandaged the itch on her hand, and worked to unpack as much as humanly possible. All the research equipment went into the master bedroom she'd refused to use.

Saturday afternoon, Jeff turned up and installed the satellite dish, giving her access to the world again through her phone. He even stayed to help break down boxes and offered to drop them off for recycling on his way back to town. By the time Andrea, Reggie, Reggie's friend, and podcast cohost, Stu arrived, the place looked like a home.

"Wow, when you said this place was in the boonies, you weren't kidding," Andrea said stepping out of Reg's Suburban. She was dressed as Andrea always dressed—as if she might hit the runway at any moment. Louboutin heels, pantsuit and matching cashmere scarf. Sara laughed and shook her head.

"I did say that, so why in the world did you wear heels?"

"Girl, you don't know who you might run into anytime, anywhere. This is a crazy small world."

"You've heard of Wisconsin, right?" Sara said. "Serial killers, cheese—"

"The Green Bay Packers."

"And what would you do with a Packer anyway?" Sara chided.

"They don't need to know I play for the other team. Just 'cause I like girls doesn't make me less of a woman. I know how to fake it. And I would for a nice dinner and some jewelry." Andrea laughed; Sara rolled her eyes.

"Okay, can we not discuss my mother's sexuality?" Reggie said, coming around from the back of the truck. He put the black equipment case he was carrying down to hug Sara. "How you been, Auntie?"

"I've been better, Reg. But hey, now I got you all here."

"Is the place as spooky as we've heard?" Stu asked. Both Reg and Stu could have come right off the stage after singing in a boy band, they were that good looking. Reg was taller and thinner but Stu's muscular build and head full of voluminous curls made up for his lack of height.

"I'd like to say no but I can't. There's a lot of strange stuff going on around here that I can't quite explain. Let's get your mom out of this ridiculous outfit." Sara turned to Andrea. "Unless you think there is still a chance of a celebrity sighting?" Andrea shook her head. "Then I'll give you a tour of the property and all things spooky."

The boys studied the wall mural and the lake monster while Andrea changed clothes. Sara stayed quiet and let them talk it out together. After all, they were the weird history experts.

Stu pointed to the monster. "This creature was painted on after the original mural was done and by a less talented artist, I'd say."

Reggie nodded. "Uh huh. For sure."

"I suspected a different artist did the monster," Sara acknowledged. "It was a commune, so that's not surprising. In fact, the idea that it was only one artist would be a more radical idea than multiple. But what makes you think it was not all done around the same time?"

"For instance, see here: the monster is a pink-peach color which is an odd choice for this particular style of art in the first place. Psychedelic art used a lot of primary and bright colors. So, a light pink or peach hue—what a white girl like yourself might call flesh tone—is out of place here." Stu gave her a friendly punch in the arm. "But also, its thicker and hasn't faded as much. Here, come touch it."

Sara obliged. The paint had been applied thicker. "But it would have to be thicker if it was painted on top of the mural and thicker means lasts longer, right?"

"Don't let him get to your head, Auntie," Reg said. "He's an art history freshman, he don't know jack shit." This earned another arm punch from Stu, but Reggie got it harder than Sara.

"I think the creature might be real." Sara said. There, it was out. And it sounded just as crazy as it had in her head.

"What?" the boys asked in unison.

68

"What's real?" Andrea asked coming down the stairs.

"Swamp Thing," Stu answered. "Check it out. Sara says it's real and not just the product of some freaky acid trip."

"For God sakes, Sara. You really have lost it up here. You think there's a swamp thing living in the lake?"

"I don't know what it is but there is something alive in that lake."

"Bill will be thrilled. He was worried there wouldn't be anything exciting for him here," Andrea said referring to the other biologist coming to research the animal life.

"Let's go see it," Reg said. "If you don't mind, Auntie."

Walking out the back door and to the lake, Reg and Stu discussed using the mural as a backdrop for the podcast and video recording. Stu made everyone stop so he could run back for the go-pro camera, "in case we see anything."

"You have to toss something in to wake it up," Sara said, realizing how ridiculous she sounded. *Maybe I really am losing my mind. Maybe Phil's death and the move and the history of the place is all swirling around in my head and screwing with my neurons.*

"There's no rocks or anything here," Andrea said. She bent down and dug her fingers into the soil.

"I know. I threw in my wedding ring the time I actually saw the thing."

"Ha!" Andrea yelled and gave Sara a fist bump.

"What exactly did you see?" Reg asked gently. *He thinks I'm crazy, too.*

"I saw a pale face. I threw the ring, and I was just sort of looking in the water and a pale face came up from the depths and looked right at me. It wasn't my reflection, either." She decided to nip that argument in the bud immediately.

"Whoa, dude," Stu said. "Maybe it was like that fish with the human face. Did you guys see that online? Creepy as shit." It was Reggie's turn to hit Stu.

"Could have been a turtle. Like you saw the shell shaped like a human face...'bout the right size, too," Reg offered.

"It wasn't green or dark. It was white. Very pale."

Andrea wandered over to the west side of the lake to inspect the swampy area. She called back, "Marsh is right for turtles. Could have been an albino or an older one with a damaged shell."

"Maybe it was a snapper!" Stu pinched Reg hard in the butt and laughed.

"Pareidolia," Andrea announced.

"What's that?" Sara asked straining her brain for the familiar word's meaning. Without context, it could have been the scientific name for a specific turtle or the medical term for the type of insanity Sara was suffering.

"Seeing faces in inanimate objects. Our mind does that all the time. We're programmed to look for facial patterns. It's survival level stuff."

Sara felt like an idiot. Of course, it could have been a turtle. Andrea was right. The marshy, swampy land was right there. But then again, "What would it have survived on? Everything here is dead."

"Life, uh, finds a way," Stu said. This time, Sara hit him in the arm.

"You mentioned there was some new growth recently?" Andrea asked. Sara had. She'd sent an email with updates and the GPS coordinates after Jeff installed her Wi-Fi.

"Oh, yeah. Around the house some new vines are coming up and out by the shed there are some mushrooms, too."

"Show me," Andrea said. They left the guys puzzling over what to throw into the water and headed to the side of the house.

There were no shoots, no vines, in fact nothing green at all along the edge of the house.

"I don't get it. I was just here two days ago and they were growing. The dish guy even mentioned it." Before waiting for Andrea's response, Sara beelined to the greenhouses. The mushrooms were gone, too. Everything was dead, just as it had been when she'd arrived.

She heard Andrea's slow steps coming up behind her and she worked to stave off her tears. Instead of speaking, Andrea wrapped her arms around Sara and held her. Sara broke and allowed herself to cry.

"You're tired, you're stressed, and you're all alone in a creepy house with a creepy mural of a creepy monster. You've got a creepy old man as a neighbor and everyone in town wants to tell you all about the creepy hippies who used to live here. It's not surprising that you think you see things or that your dreams and memories are getting mixed up," Andrea said still holding her. Sara wriggled out of her grasp and turned around.

"Is that what you think? That I've dreamed all this up? Andrea! I *saw* something in the lake, and I threw Phil's urn in as well."

"You did what? No, Sara. You shouldn't have done that."

"It's fine. I threw it in the lake and then later, it was back on my table and there were muddy wet footprints in my kitchen. Whatever is out there brought it back."

"Sara. Listen to yourself. You know there cannot be some humanoid sea creature out there just bringing back anything you thoughtlessly threw into the lake. Come on."

"Okay, I know how this sounds. But something keeps coming in the house. Something stole the food you sent me, and I've heard it scratching at the basement door. I've seen it moving behind the keyhole." She lowered her voice. "I saw it watching me."

"Well, have you looked in the basement? If there is anything here, Sara, it's probably some homeless bum. Maybe it's the crazy neighbor, but there is no monster."

She felt like a child. "You're right. You're right. I thought there might be a squatter, too. But the door is locked and Stephanie, the realtor, doesn't have a key. I don't want to damage the door, so I haven't done anything more with it."

"Let's go have a look. Maybe Reggie or Stu can get in. Those boys have picked their share of locks getting into places they have no business getting into for that dumb show of theirs."

The boys had given up on the lake monster and were unloading the car and setting up their studio when Andrea and Sara came back to the house.

"Reg, come help us open this basement door," Andrea said, grabbing her son's arm and pulled him through the living room. Stu sprawled under their folding table, plugging wires into equipment and taping them down to the thin carpet.

"What's up with you not having a key? Didn't you buy this place?" Reggie asked Sara.

"Yes, but the door is locked and, somewhere along the line, someone lost the only key. I can't bear to damage the door; it's original."

"She's been hearing things scratching at it and she thinks there is someone living in the basement. A bum or something," Andrea told him. Sara wished she hadn't. She was already feeling like such a fool, no need to let the guys know just how paranoid she'd become.

"No kidding? Well, if that's so, then they got the key. The way these locks work, you can lock and unlock from either side, you just need the key. It's the only way to do it, so if it is locked, and someone is coming in through this door…" Reggie grabbed the knob and turned as if to prove the bum on the other side was locking it.

The door swung open easily. Graying wooden steps appeared in the wedge of light provided by the kitchen. Reg and Andrea looked at Sara, whose mouth was gaping like a lake monster out of water. She shook her head in disbelief.

"It was locked. I must have tried it a thousand times. It's been locked the whole time."

"Then I think it's time we go down there and find the motherfucker who's been fucking with your head," her best friend said. "Stu! Come in here." Then to Reg. "You carrying?"

He lifted up his untucked shirt to show her his pistol strapped securely in its holster. He flicked open the strap with his thumb and nodded.

"You and Stu go first, if it's clear, holler and we'll come down. Enough of this shit." Andrea looked at Sara. "I know you're not crazy, honey. I know that. Someone's playing with you. Maybe this town's got a secret they don't want us to know. Maybe you do have a squatter. Whatever it is, that's what we're here to discover, and I'm not leaving you alone again until we do. You got that? I believe you."

The women watched the boys descend into the mysterious underground. A light broke the darkness followed by an "Oh shit" which broke the silence.

Sara and Andrea waited, holding their breath, listening for the sounds of a fight or, god-forbid, a gunshot. "Jackpot!" Reggie yelled laughing. Sara and Andrea looked at each other before running down to see what they'd found.

Shelves lined both sides of the room at the bottom of the stairs. Most were bare, but some held unlabeled jars of jam-like substances and bottles of mead made and stored over forty years ago. Reggie had two bottles of mead in his hands, arms held in the air in victory.

"If you got a bum living down here," Stu said to Sara as she took in the scene, "the guy's an idiot. What kind of bum doesn't go for liquor?"

"The non-human kind," Andrea said. She'd walked around Sara and into the room to the right of the stairs. Hairs on the back of Sara's neck stood at attention and chills retreated from the top of her head down to her hands. She shivered and willed herself into the room where, presumably, Andrea had found some evidence of the lake creature.

The room Andrea found was filled with rotting mattresses, mildewed blankets and clothes, empty glass bottles, and a myriad of trash. Ancient wooden shelves leaned against dirt walls in this room as well—only there was nothing on them. Besides remnants of a lost commune, Sara saw nothing that would indicate anything non-human lived here.

"What?" she asked.

Andrea pointed to the shelves. "Raccoons, maybe groundhogs? I don't know, maybe a badger or something. Bill will know."

Behind and between the boards, Sara saw them immediately. Tunnels. Big holes in the walls that opened up into the room.

Raccoons. That explained the missing food, the scratching and pawing at the door. But not the door being locked and unlocked. Not the eye that looked just like hers in the keyhole. She thought about arguing that point, but decided against it. The more she insisted, the crazier she sounded.

"Mystery solved. I feel a lot better. Thanks." She tried to smile but the best she could do was to hold back the tears.

"Come on. This place is making us all a little nutty. Let's go check out the town and have some dinner. I'm starving." Andrea put her arm around Sara.

"When we get back, we can sample the goods," Stu said, grabbing two bottles of mead for himself.

Chapter 13

The only place Sara knew to go was Slim's, and that was just fine, because she'd come to like the middle-American diner feel of the place. Besides, there was a good chance Stephanie, her grandparents, or Julie and Roger would be there. Reggie and Stu could do some interviewing before they recorded the episode.

No one in the place was familiar, yet every head turned and stayed fixed on the group until they'd been seated and had menus in their hands.

"No one here ever seen a black man before?" Stu asked.

"Nah, they're used to white hobo kids dancing under the full moon. Our kind's a bit too strange for this town," Reggie said a little louder than necessary.

"Oh, it's me they're staring at. Everyone wants to know what I'm doing with the Demeter House and why. They all have a general fear of the place. I think the disappearance of the whole clan followed by the death of the land up there was great rumor fodder until the death started seeping downhill. Did you see the fingers spreading into Kumpula farms? They don't trust anything having to do with the commune, you know?"

"Well, the curious lady who bought the haunted house of death just brought three blacks in with her. They're really gonna lose their shit now," Andrea laughed.

"Better not tell 'em you're a lesbian, too. They'll run us out with pitchforks and torches," Stu said.

The server arrived with water for everyone and took their orders.

"So, have you got much research done on the book?" Stu asked once their drinks arrived.

"No. Stephanie took me into the newspaper to meet the owner, but he wasn't there. His wife seems pretty helpful though. She's looking through some of their archives for photos and such. I've met a couple people who lived here when the commune was in full swing, but I haven't got too much out of them."

74

"I'm not surprised," Reggie said. "From what we've been able to find, they kept to themselves. Grew walls of vines around the property, never invited outsiders in. The only time anyone saw them was during Farmers' Markets."

"Rumors though, lots of speculation about what they were doing up there," Stu added. "Man, I'd like to get into those caves!"

"Why?" Sara asked.

"Because that's where they did a lot of their worshiping and shit, I guess," Reggie answered.

"Sacrifices," Stu whispered.

Sara looked around. People still watched, only trying to be less obvious about it. "I want to hear more, but not until we get home," she said. "Now, tell me about this podcast thing."

The guys filled the conversation with exploits of the haunted or otherwise mysterious places they'd been or researched. Sara and Andrea listened and laughed. Sara tried to ignore the itching on her hand. Instead, she picked at the gauze wrapping until Andrea smacked her hand under the table.

"Don't think I didn't notice you're at it again," she whispered. "That man wasn't worth destroying a piece of toilet paper, let alone your own skin. You're finally living your dream." She squeezed her friend's hand and Sara smiled at her.

"Sara! So good to see you out and about." Stephanie appeared at the table smiling her effervescent smile.

"Oh, hey Stephanie! I was hoping you might come in. Let me introduce you to my friends. This is Andrea, her son Reggie, and his friend Stu. I think I told you Reggie and Stu are doing a podcast at the house about the Demeter clan? Tomorrow, actually. I was hoping maybe they could interview you a little about whatever you can remember."

The smile fell out of her eyes but remained on her lips. It was subtle, but Sara noticed.

"Well, I doubt I'd be much of an interview. I was only eight when they disappeared."

"Nah, anything you can remember about them would help, even if it's just that they all seemed normal," Reggie said. He was a smooth talker, that one.

"Or, maybe your grandfather or grandmother might be willing?" Sara offered.

"No. I wouldn't want to bother them with this. Townsfolk their age don't really like to talk about it. They thought the kids were all a bunch of dirty hippies to begin with, and even if they came around with their harvest, a lot of them had issues with the way they raised their kids and all the free love and whatnot. They'll start speculating about things they know nothing about, and that kind of talk gets Grandad all riled up. His blood pressure doesn't need that sort of stressor."

"Oh sure, no worries. Has he ever speculated to you? I mean about what he thought they were up to?" Stu pressed.

"You know, anything I tell you would be hearsay on a bunch of theories. Children of Demeter were peaceful farmers. So what if they were pagans and worshipped a different deity than most? They worked very hard, and they sacrificed for their harvests, which they sold as a means to provide for themselves. What's so wrong with that?"

"Speaking of sacrifices, have you ever heard rumors that they performed human sacrifices up there? Babies or kids?" Stu asked.

Stephanie pulled a chair from an empty table and dragged it between Andrea and Sara.

"Sure. That's what they did. They sacrificed babies. Just tossed 'em in the lake or down the well. Sometimes they left them for dead in the caves."

Reggie and Stu's eyes bulged wide enough that Sara could see the whites all the way around their irises.

"She's being sarcastic, you two idiots," Andrea said.

Ignoring the rebuke, Reggie tried a question. "Stephanie, what do you think happened to them all? I mean, one day they were there and the next day, they were gone."

"Isn't that what hippies do? They travel, they don't keep many possessions. I think they probably got wind of another call to CPS or something and left in the night."

"But what about their van and that pickup? Why wouldn't they take their vehicles?" Stu asked.

"Probably broke down. I don't know. Maybe they hitched."

"I have a hard time believing that. What, twenty-some young adults and children just walked out of town in the middle of the night and not a single soul saw anything?" Sara couldn't accept what sounded like pure nonsense coming from a woman she regarded as a friend and someone she thought of as intelligent.

"Well, if you want to know what I think, I think some people *do* know. I think some of those kids maybe belonged to some men in town. Maybe some married men. I think someone, or maybe a few someones, helped them leave. Maybe under threat or maybe one of the daddies felt guilty enough to get them out before CPS showed up."

"Before the baby mamas started naming names you mean," Andrea quipped. "I see where you're going and that makes a lot of sense. Only thing I don't understand is why, if they were such devoted followers of an earth goddess, they would poison the land? And I mean, they did something big, right? So big that, forty years later, the land is still sterile, and now it's leaching outward like a slow growing cancer. I've never even heard of a poison that could do that."

"Maybe it wasn't them." Stephanie shrugged.

Chapter 14

Andrea slept in the next morning, blaming the long drive and the "stress of small-town living" when Sara tried to rouse her. Regardless, Sara dragged the guys out to the cement slab as soon as they were up and moving.

"What's this symbol about?" Reggie asked.

"I don't know. It's on the baluster, too."

"There's something similar on the mural near Swamp Thing." Stu traced the outline with his finger. "Maybe this is where they keep the beast they fed the babies to?"

"Enough, sicko," Reggie said. "Let's see if we can move this off here and have a look."

Together, the two nudged the unwieldy slab about three inches off its base.

"You need a crowbar," Roy Kumpula said. All three spun around. The old man held one up. He'd come prepared.

"You're trespassing," Sara said matter of factly.

"Guess I am. But you don't seem to take too well to warnings. If you can't beat 'em, join 'em, they say." He turned his attention to Reggie and Stu. "Which one of you two wanna work this thing? I'll help push."

"No!" Sara stepped between Roy and the boys. "I don't want you here."

"Darlin', you got me all wrong. All I'm trying to do is keep you safe. This place isn't good for anybody, but especially not for you."

"What does that mean?" Sara put her hands on her hips and refused to move. "And do not patronize me with that 'darlin'' nonsense."

Roy chuckled and shook his head. "Stubborn and feisty. I should have expected that." He stepped around her and handed the bar to Stu. "Let's get the lid off this thing, boys. She wants to know everything? Well, then, sooner the better."

Sara was too shocked to say anything else. Besides, Stu had already accepted the crowbar. The three men shoved off the lid. Decades-old must of rotting vegetation and dampness wafted up from the deep earth.

"Whew!" Reggie backed away from the hole and waved his hand in front of his face. "Who knew air could hold on to stink for such a long time?"

Stu took his phone with the flashlight app on, and directed the light into the hole. "I can't see anything."

"I'd say it's pretty deep. Doubt you'll see the bottom. Probably for the best." Roy tossed a quarter in. They all listened but were unsatisfied with the uncertainty of its landing. Sara thought she heard the soft thud of it hitting bottom, but she could've just as easily imagined it.

"Did it hit?" Stu asked. Reggie shrugged.

"Sorry for trespassing. I hope you find the answers you're looking for before you end up getting hurt. You seem like a fine person." Roy picked up his crowbar and headed back toward his field.

"Hey, hey, hold up," Reggie said. He reached out and touched the old man's shoulder. "My friend and I co-host a podcast about mysterious places. We're recording one tonight on The Children of Demeter clan. We have mostly background and speculation to talk about, but I bet you've got a lot you could tell us, having lived right next to them."

"No," Sara interrupted. "I want him gone. You can't trust him, and I want him gone. He is not coming in my home."

"*Your* home?" Roy muttered.

"That's right, it is my home, not yours." He needed to understand, so he could let go of the idea that he would ever own Demeter house.

"Come on, Auntie. We got nothing without him. Just the mural with the lake monster—"

"You uncovered the mural?" Roy interrupted.

"You know about that?" Stu asked excitedly. "You gotta help us out, dude."

"You've been inside my house." It wasn't a question.

"Not any time recently." Roy held up his hands in a gesture of innocent surrender.

"You see?" Sara said to the boys. "He's a crazy stalker. I don't want him inside my home."

"Please, Auntie? We'll be there with him the whole time."

"Don't know anything about podcasts, only know about casting a fishin' line. Plus, I hate to upset the young lady."

Sara took in the strange man. He knew about the mural. He was there when the clan was at its peak. Wasn't she writing a book about them? Didn't *she* need the information as much as the guys? If Roy had anything pertinent to say, why not get it on record? She could refer to it later and never have to sit down with him alone to do an interview.

The farmer was surely strong, but he was old. The guys could take him, if he tried anything. She didn't think he would, though. He was the sneaky type. He was up to something, of that she had no doubt, but what exactly, she didn't know. It might be her chance to figure him out.

"Fine. He can do the podcast, but then…" She turned to face the old man. "I don't want to see you around here again. Do you understand?"

"I'd like to ask the same of you."

Chapter 15

Podcast Transcript

Intro: Welcome to another episode of *The Mysterious Creepcast*, where your hosts Reg and Stu are creepin' it real with true tales of strange places. Come on in…if you dare.

Reggie: Hey, hey. It's your buds Reggie and Stu, back for another trip into the creepy and mysterious world we live in.

Stu: That's right, this shit is the real deal, my friends. We don't play around. Each week, we broadcast live from haunted, cursed, or otherwise fucked up places where all sorts of weird shit happened.

Reggie: This week, we're coming at you from West Burma, Wisconsin. A tiny little village in southwest Wisconsin, which used to be the home of The Children of Demeter clan. From 1968 to 1973, this commune of self-proclaimed pagan earth worshippers—

Stu: Basically, a bunch of hippies.

Reggie: Yeah, it was a hippie commune. Mostly runaways and vagabonds in their late teens and early twenties. They settled here in the very house we're broadcasting from. They called themselves The Children of Demeter and declared themselves devout followers and worshippers of the deity Demeter. Stu, what did you find about Demeter?

Stu: Well, Demeter is the Greek goddess of the harvest and fertility of the Earth. She presided over the cycle of life and death and the laws of nature. She is best known as the mother of Persephone who was kidnapped by Hades and taken to the underworld. Demeter searched for her daughter endlessly and, while doing that, the seasons halted and living things stopped growing and died. Ultimately, in the Greek mythos, Zeus had to step in and tell Hades to bring Persephone back before all of life went extinct.

Reggie: But didn't Hades trick her somehow and get to keep her for like some of the year?

Stu: Yeah, that's the whole pomegranate thing. Hades gave Persephone a pomegranate and, when she ate some of it, it bound her to him so that she had to return to him once a year. That's when Demeter mourns her daughter's loss and things die. Like, that explains winter, I guess.

Reggie: Okay, so that whole myth is important to this story, given what happened here in the fall of 1973 then, wouldn't you say, Stu?

Stu: Yeah—it's crazy, but it sure seems like The Children of Demeter knew the history of their goddess well.

Reggie: So, let's get into the story of The Children of Demeter, then we'll introduce our guest.

Stu: Sure. So, in 1966 or '67 this guy who called himself Esmond Light set up shop here and started gathering a following. Mostly women.

Reggie: Like Manson, almost. Creepy.

Stu: Maybe, but the difference here was that Esmond did not proclaim himself a god or a messiah. He worshipped the earth and started his cult that way. We don't know much about him or any of their rituals other than to say that many people believed they were up to some weird stuff up here. Witchy stuff, maybe—naked orgies, animal sacrifices, that sort of thing.

Reggie: Well, you said she was the goddess of fertility, didn't you?

Stu: I did, and it was no secret that the cult was fertile. There were always pregnant women at the farmer's market.

Reggie: Talk about that—they made their living selling all sorts of things from their harvest every weekend at the farmer's market in town.

Stu: Oh yeah, they were known for their jams and meads, honey, vegetables, and fruits. I mean, people drove from all over to buy from them.

Reggie: Whatever they were doing to appease their goddess, it was working.

Stu: Right. But while the town and everyone around enjoyed the spoils of their harvest, many secretly had concerns about the children of the clan and their wellbeing. There was also a lot of speculation about what exactly they were doing up on the hill.

Reggie: As in, what they were doing ritualistically?

Stu: Well, that, I think, and what were they doing to get such amazing produce, when neighbors and other farmers in the area were not getting near the quality crops that they were?

Reggie: Speaking of neighbors and farmers, it might be a good time to bring in our guest. Roy Kumpula is a local farmer whose land borders the Demeter land. He's lived here all his life and had some interactions with the cult. We can go on with our research and speculations, but I think it's great to have a firsthand account.

Stu: Agreed. Welcome, Roy.

Roy: Thank you.

Reggie: So, you grew up here in West Burma?

Roy: Yessir. Born and raised.

Reggie: And your farm? You inherited that from your father?

Roy: That farm's been in my family for generations.

Reggie: Awesome. So, what do you know about The Children of Demeter? Do you know anything about this Esmond Light guy, and how he ended up settling in West Burma?

Stu: Right? I mean didn't most hippies head west to California? Wisconsin winters would be tough for a bunch of broke kids.

Roy: This house used to be owned—was built, I think—by a German couple. Schmidt was their name. They had about six kids or so. 'Course none of them wanted to stick around and help, so Schmidt sold most of the land to my dad. Kept a small square for their own garden, the orchard, the greenhouses. The old lady was a wiz with plants.

Reggie: What about the caves and the mucky field? Who owns that?

Roy: Oh yeah, that's part of this land. It wasn't muck and marsh back then. Was a solid field. Schmidt kept that and the caves—believe he wanted to do some cheesemaking. Had a deal with Dad to get the milk from our cows. Never got around to it, though. Had a heart attack not long after he sold his plot of land to my family.

Stu: Then the old lady sold the place to Esmond?

Roy: Nope. *Esmond* was their grandson. Real name was Rolf. Rolf came

Stu: You were in Vietnam? Shit, man, I'm sorry. How long?

Roy: Two years, would've stayed the whole time, seen it through 'til the bitter end, 'cept my daddy had a stroke, and I was all they had. My brother died when he was eight. Influenza. Got shipped home to manage the family farm and care for him and my mom.

Reggie: So, when you got back, Rolf had become Esmond Light and had his commune in full swing, I'm guessing?

Roy: Oh yeah. Full swing. Mrs. Schmidt was dead and buried. Rolf had, oh, I'd say about a dozen, maybe fifteen people living there? Most of 'em girls. Up singing and dancing all hours of the night, bonfires, screaming babies.

Reggie: Screaming babies?

Roy: Girls were always pregnant, never knew whose kid was whose. Little naked toddlers running around all snot-nosed. Babies in wraps sucking on a tit here and then someone else's tit later. Crying all day and night.

Reggie: Did you ever see anything suspicious? You know what I'm getting at? Sacrifices. You say babies and kids crying. You know the stories.

Roy: I know what you're getting at, and I couldn't tell ya. When Rolf moved in, he put up a bunch of wooden spikes—not sharp, more like a bunch of tall sapling trunks—along the border of our land. When I got home, they had a wall of thick ivy grown up so that you couldn't see much of anything they were up to.

Stu: Do you thinks it's possible they were up to anything strange or illegal?

Roy: Possible. As you said, they sure did have the sweetest fruits and best produce. Don't know how they did it. All organic—no pesticides, no chemicals. Just good, all-natural food straight from the earth. Kept bees, in fact, had a bunch of clover in that field where's now it's all mud.

Reggie: Roy, I'm going to challenge you a little here. For those of you watching the video, you can see the background is a painted-over mural. We're in what we're calling Demeter House, and our friend who now owns it has been excavating this mural that was covered over with paint. As you can see, she's exposed what seems to be a mural depicting the land and house with one interesting addition. This lake creature, here.

Stu: Swamp Thing!

Reggie: Roy, when we were talking to you earlier before the show, you seemed to know about this mural.

Roy: Uh huh. Been in here once or twice before. I was young and back from the war. Curious to have myself a gander at the young, nubile, and most of the time, naked girls. Used to take a break from plowing and do a little monitoring through the ivy vines. Been home for a couple years when I saw a girl caught my eye. Started spending a lot more time peering through the ivy 'stead of working on the fields. Wasn't long before she noticed me watching her. Called herself Merry, spelled it like Christmas. We got to talking. Sweet girl, but real loyal to the cult. Well, what they called themselves was The Children of Demeter, like you said.

Stu: Did she see it as a cult? I mean, I always wonder what the people on the inside are thinking.

Roy: Some days, when Rolf was off doing whatever he did to bring in new members, we'd sit, and she would explain to me how Demeter and Mother Earth and Gaia were all the same and she'd say things like how their commune was awakening the earth. How, if they worshipped her and gave back to her, Demeter would bring back paradise on earth— like the Garden of Eden, was how she put it.

Reggie: That seems to be about what they were doing from what I understand. I hear this place was pretty lush in its heyday, and you, like everyone else we've talked to, agree that their produce was otherworldly.

Roy: Pretty much. Merry said that, as long as they kept the goddess happy, they were rewarded.

Stu: What did they have to do to keep her happy?

Roy: Don't know. She wouldn't tell me. I asked often, but she said it wasn't something to be shared outside the group.

Reggie: And she never invited you to join or asked Esmond if you could?

Roy: She took me out to the caves once. They were using a couple of 'em for fermenting their mead, but the one she took me into had an altar of sorts. Had piles of wheat and jars of honey and mead on it. Candles lit up all over. There was a bunch of rolled up rag rugs along the wall and she took one down, laid it out. She went to the altar and gathered up some fruit and mead, and we ate and drank and got naked.

Stu: Yeah, Roy! Were you scared she was gonna sacrifice you?

Roy: She dug her fingers into the mud and used it to draw all sorts of symbols on our bodies. Like the one on your cement well out there. Like the one up on the wall there.

Stu: Oh shit, man! Did she, like, call the creature of the lake out to you or something?

Roy: No. Nothing like that ever happened. We just uh…made love. Don't know how many times or even how long we were in that cave. Might have been hours, might have been days. I don't know. Lost all sense of things.

Reggie: So, let's get back to this mural and the monster that's in it. You said you've been in the house before. You've seen this mural—like before someone painted over it?

Roy: Yeah, I saw it not long after bein' with Merry in the caves. After that, see, Merry wasn't outside much. I never saw her, and when I did, if she saw me, she'd head straight back inside. When I'd had enough, figured maybe she was in trouble or something for being with me. I just marched over there one day and let myself in. That's when I saw the mural.

Stu: Did you find her? Was she okay? What did you say about the monster?

Roy: I found her. Or at least I found the room she was in. She wouldn't come out. Said she didn't want to see me ever again and not to come back.

Reggie: So, what did you do?

Roy: I left.

Stu: Did you ask anyone about the monster?

Roy: There was no monster on the painting to ask about.

Chapter 16

Andrea came downstairs just before the podcast started, and she and Sara sat on the couch listening. The boys were naturals on the mics. Sara enjoyed their banter. Roy stood off to the side waiting to be invited. Sara tried not to stare but noted Roy's eyes investigating every inch of the house that they could from their vantage point.

"I don't like the looks of that guy," Andrea whispered.

"No. Neither do I. That's the one I told you about. I think he's been sneaking around the property."

"Maybe he stole your food. If he's been around since the beginning, he might even have a key to the basement. Great place to hide, if you came home while he was snooping."

Sara hadn't thought of that, but Andrea had a point. In fact, Roy could have been the one who painted that monster on the wall sometime before she moved in. Probably trying to scare people away.

Sure, sure. And sometimes he lurks under the water in the lake waiting to scare you. You know what you saw. There is something in that lake. And, she supposed, if Roy was trying to hide in the basement, why go to the trouble to make noise and draw her attention?

Because he is trying to scare you. Yes, for sure he was trying to scare her. He more or less admitted to it out at the well. But maybe he had a good reason. Nothing made sense. It was as if she knew the answer but all the other possibilities were swirling around in her head so she couldn't nail it down. As if the whole thing—Roy, the monster, the squatter in the basement, even the house itself and the grounds around it—was part of one big jigsaw puzzle, and the box cover with the picture of how it all fit together was somewhere in her mind. She just couldn't bring it to the foreground.

"Something's certainly sketchy about him—the way he keeps looking around the house, like he is waiting for something to happen," Sara said.

The guys invited Roy to talk, and he'd sat down with them. The old farmer looked out of place and uncomfortable with the big headphones covering his ears and leaning into the microphone they'd given him. At first his answers were stiff and wooden, but gradually he became more comfortable.

"He's holding back," Sara whispered to Andrea. "Taking each question, rolling it around in his head before answering."

Andrea nodded. Roy told the boys about Merry and her take on the cult. Sara listened with budding interest as he described how the cult believed that Demeter, Mother Earth, and Gaia were all the same. Sara's father was a world literature professor who specialized in Greek Mythology. Growing up, Sara had been fascinated with the stories about the gods and goddesses and how they interacted with mortals. In ancient cults, Gaia and Demeter were often worshipped together. Gaia, though separate from Demeter, gave birth to the Titans, the primordial pre-gods. Some considered them monsters. She looked at the mural again, taking in the humanoid creature depicted near the lake. Could that be a representation of a Titan? She made a mental note to look into Rolf Schmidt's upbringing and education.

Andrea leaned forward, totally immersed in Roy's tale. Sara, still dubious of the man, put on her sociologist's cap and tried to pick up telltale pauses or abrupt shifts that would signify he was holding back or altogether lying.

"We need to get into those caves," Sara whispered, but Andrea held up a hand to shush her. Roy's story was more than any of them had gotten from anyone else. He had been inside the cult, had interacted with at least one of its members. Sara wanted to retrace those steps.

The pregnant pause after Roy told them there had been no monster in the original mural was lengthy. Reggie, to his credit, proceeded as if nothing had surprised him and the pause was for the audience to take in.

Reggie: Wow, interesting. So, did you ever see Merry again?

Roy: No.

Stu: So…that's it?

Roy: That's it.

Reggie: What happened to them, Roy? You met Merry, what, in '71 or '72? And by '73, they were gone. All of them. For you folks at home, The Children of Demeter cult disappeared overnight on September 26, 1973. Not a single body was found. Their truck and all their belongings were left behind.

Stu: To add weird to freaky, everything around the place went dead. All the vegetation, the greenhouses were found destroyed, and the lake was devoid of life. No fish, no seaweed, no cattails. The clover fields had turned to muck, the ivy covering the house gone brown and dry.

Reggie: And nothing, not a single thing, has grown here since. Something else, too, the deadness—if that's even a word—has started to spread, like a rash, into your land, your fields, Roy. Isn't that right?

Roy: Yep. That's true.

Reggie: Care to make a guess as to what might be going on?

Roy: Demeter's lookin' for her lost daughter.

Reggie: I think that's the best answer we have at the moment. Roy, thank you so much for sharing your story with us. Here's my card, man. If you think of anything else, give me a call, we'd love to have you back.

Roy: Sure will.

Outro: Come find us next week where all things are lost and everything's creepy. Until then, Reg and Stu are ghosts.

Chapter 17

The man was insane. If he thought that Demeter was a real deity causing everything that had happened, then he might truly be a dangerous psychopath. What if he was the one poisoning the land all this time? What if he—*what, Sara? What if he what? Killed them all? Somehow slaughtered two dozen people and hid the crime so well that no one has ever discovered it? Maybe* you're *the dangerous psychopath.*

No matter. The guys were thrilled with their podcast and took the video camera out to film some of the locations discussed in the episode for bonus material. Roy, as promised, bid everyone farewell, walked into his cornfield, and disappeared.

"I still don't trust the guy," Sara said. She watched until the last bit of blue from his ballcap disappeared.

"Oh, he's not so bad," Andrea countered.

"Not so bad? Did you hear him say the land is dead because Demeter is searching for her daughter? Really?"

"My God, Sara! He was joking. That's the Demeter story, right? Persephone with Hades in the underworld, the land above in hibernation while Demeter mourns?" Andrea took Sara's hand and held it between her own. "Hey, I know it's been rough lately. You've had to take in and process so much with Phil and Marie and his death. You had to just move on without answers. Then you leave town and come here—to another situation filled with more questions, more unknowns, and still no answers. You've got this weird neighbor who seems to be trying to scare you away. You've got some kind of creature living in your basement scaring the bejeezus out of you. It's no wonder you're filled with mistrust."

"You make it sound like I'm being unreasonable."

"Well, I don't mean to. I think everything you've been thinking and feeling is reasonable *under the circumstances.*" She patted Sara's hand for emphasis. "Now, I think, when the boys get back, we should celebrate a successful visit. You got as much information for your book as they did for the podcast. You have something to focus on after we leave and before Bill, the students, and I come back. It's all good."

Sara nodded. There would be no more arguing her side. When Bill and the students came with Andrea, and they all settled in, when the research started to stir up all the strange things, then they would see. They would see the thing in the lake, and they would hear the thing behind the basement door. They would finally realize that the place was, indeed, coming back to life.

"Well," she said, following Andrea's plan. "How do you propose we celebrate?"

"With Demeter mead of course!" She laughed and took off into the kitchen as if they were racing to the basement.

They spent the rest of the night drinking and laughing around a fire they'd built in the backyard. The reflection of the stars on the lake danced and twinkled when a breeze ruffled the water. Subconsciously, Sara hoped the monster would rise up from the depths of the lake and terrify the group, even if it meant her own demise. At least for a few moments, she would be vindicated. She listened behind them, waiting for the screen door to creak and something else—maybe a crazed killer or another creature—to come out of its hiding place in the house and eat them up.

"I have an idea," Stu said as if reading her mind. "What about one of those night vision wildlife cameras? You know, the kind hunters use to get pictures of deer they want to shoot or something. I don't know what exactly the point of them is, but, like, I think you just set it up, and it's, like, motion activated. Maybe you can get pics of the monster."

"Could set one up in the kitchen, too," Andrea added. "Catch your raccoon or whatever it is."

"It's not a bad idea," Sara agreed. Certainly, if the creatures were not going to cooperate by coming to their impromptu party, she could still have some sort of proof that they existed.

"It's a great idea," Stu corrected.

"Now, if only one of us can remember it tomorrow." Reggie poured more mead into everyone's glasses. Andrea put a hand out over her own.

"Sorry, guys. All this fresh air and country living has me tuckered out. Sara, don't forget, we're old now. We can't hang with these young pups. Don't stay out too late." She hugged her friend and ruffled Reggie's hair before heading inside.

The "young pups" waited until Andrea left to offer Sara a joint. She declined but downed her glass of mead and poured another.

The more she drank, the more alert she became to the sounds and shadows around her. The mead worked itself into her veins and spread like vines until she felt them crawling along her skin on the outside as well. The earth caressed her and called her into its bosom. The chatter of the others became background noise, like the call of cicadas, as Mother Earth whispered her secrets to Sara.

She was a child of Demeter. She belonged there. In the house, on the land. She was fertile and sexual. She could grow and become something new within this womb. Sara got up from her chair slowly, so as not to break the fragile, unseen tendrils that blanketed her. She walked to the lake, peeling clothes off as she went.

"Hey, hey, hey Auntie. Put these back on." Reg rushed behind her with her clothes he'd gathered as he followed.

Stu had caught up as well, and he grabbed her by the arm, slowing her progress toward the lake. "Where ya going, Sara? I'm not sure this lake is the best place for skinny dipping. How 'bout you come back to the house with us?"

Stu's touch on her arm spilled through her like tea, warming her core and flooding her delta. She spun and fell fully into his arms then kissed him.

"Auntie!" Reg came to them, but when he touched Sara, the warmth within her pulsed, pulling him in as it had Stu. She pushed his head down and let him fall to his knees where he, like Stu, could worship her with his mouth.

The frenzy went on for some time. Sara only knew her body was being used in the way it was meant to be. Doing what nature intended, as all creatures to do.

"What the fuck is going on here?" Andrea screamed. She came at them with arms flailing. Hitting and kicking until the trio broke up, panting like dogs in heat.

"Sara, Goddamn. That's my boy! That's my son!" Andrea huffed out of breath. "And you," she pointed at Reggie. "She might as well be your mom. She helped raise you. What…? I mean…I have no words. This is sickening, is what it is!"

Sara said nothing. She felt nothing. She stood and walked past Andrea without a word. Into the house. In her room, in her house, on her land, she slept a dreamless and contented sleep.

Chapter 18

Sara awoke to noises that sounded like a houseful of horses. She had no memory of the night before. *Must have been the mead.* She happily discovered she had no hangover and made a mental note that mead was her new drink of choice. The front door slammed and Sara jumped. She hadn't gotten around to plugging in her alarm clock—her old-school ass couldn't give it up, even if she had a smart phone. The door slammed again and then again. No time to dig around in her purse for the cell, it was probably dead anyway.

She pulled on a pair of jogging pants and a tee shirt then thumped down the stairs. Andrea reentered as she did. Her friend let the door swing shut hard then glared at her.

"Uh, good morning to you, too?" Sara said confused.

"It will be a good morning when I don't have to look at your whore-face," Andrea answered and shouldered past her.

"What?" Sara followed after her. The podcast setup had been torn down, and there was no sign of the boys anywhere. "Hey!" Sara caught up with her in the kitchen. "What is going on, Andrea?"

Andrea, who had poured herself a glass of wine then chugged it down like cold beer on a hot day, tossed the empty glass into the sink without wincing when it shattered. She put her hands on her hips and glared at Sara. She squinted her eyes and searched Sara's face for some sign of what, Sara didn't know.

"The boys say you were in some sort of trance, sleepwalking or something. Maybe so. But," her voice rose to a furious screech. "I cannot erase the vision of my best friend and my son fucking like wild animals in the back yard! Not to mention seeing my son's best friend right there with you both!"

Sara's stomach dropped to her knees, and they buckled under the weight. She grabbed the closest chair and leaned hard on it. Andrea's words sucked all the air from the room, and Sara felt her mouth gape like a fish.

"Yeah, I see. Well, I don't know what is going on with you in this house, Sara. I don't know, but I think we've solved the mystery of the stolen food and the footprints and the returned urn. It's *you*. You're doing this. Don't bother wasting your money on a game cam. You'll just embarrass yourself."

"Andrea, I truly, truly do not remember last night. I would never willingly or knowingly come on to your son. Never! You know me. He's like my own son. How do you think I could—"

"I *saw* it, Sara." She pointed at her eyes; fingers so close Sara thought her friend might pluck them out. "I saw everything." Andrea covered her face and began to cry.

"Oh God, I don't know what to say. I'm sorry. I'm so, so sorry. This place, it gets under my skin." As soon as the words were out, her hand began itching. It was maddening. Sara tried to ignore it, tried to focus on her breathing, and her friend, but the itch bit at her like a thousand tiny ants.

"I should apologize to Reg and Stu," Sara said, thinking she could sneak away and scratch at the biting itch.

"No! I told them they are to have no contact with you. Leave them alone. They are just as confused as you are."

"Well…" Sara rubbed on the bandage. "That has to tell you something. We're all confused. Maybe it was the mead, maybe it was—" She was going to say "maybe it was the pot," but decided the poor boys were in enough trouble as it was. "I don't know. But what you saw," Andrea flinched. "It wasn't us. You must know that."

Andrea stood and wiped away the tears with the back of her wrist. "Do me a favor, Sara. Go see a doctor. Get on some medication before Bill and I bring students here. Please."

"Of course. I guess I didn't realize how much Phil's death affected me. I thought I could run away from it."

"You can't run away from yourself," Andrea said. "I'll see you in a couple weeks."

Sara conceded. Andrea grabbed her purse from the table and walked out.

Ripping off the gauze, Sara tore into the flesh on her hand. The relief was no different than finally peeing after having to hold it so long it hurt. As a college professor, she'd had many opportunities to feel that sort of discomfort too. She wanted to think about the night before, wanted to retrace her memories of the entire evening—but first, the itch.

When the pain overcame the compulsion to scratch, she stopped. The previously un-assaulted skin around the healing wound turned red and wept. She wrapped the gauze around again, determined to forget about it. She wanted to forget everything else, too, but she couldn't cover up Andrea's accusations with a bandage.

Meandering back into the living room, she plopped down on the couch and pondered the mural, the lake, the house, the ancient goddess, and the disappearance of an entire clan of her worshippers. The idea that underneath the cheap paint, the mural told a tale explaining the mysteries of Demeter's Children returned to the front of her mind. If things were going to get back to normal, she had to uncover it—the entire thing—right then, before anyone else came to the house.

Using the paint scraper, she uncovered the entire house. Since she already knew about the well, she decided to see what she might find on the other side near the greenhouses and the orchard.

The fruits hanging from the trees in the colorful painting were huge, dripping with dew, and unusual. Figs, perhaps, maybe pears, but they grew upside down like giant uteruses. Seeds fell from some of the fruit, and where they hit the ground, tiny children sprung forth from the soil. By the greenhouses, Wonderland-sized mushrooms grew and shaded half a large pomegranate. Its seeds spilled out and over the sides like bubbles over a cauldron.

The greenhouses themselves appeared to be struggling to hold back the verdant tentacles of vines that pierced through every window and crevice growing in all directions, writhing and grasping at any solid object for support. The psychedelic swirls provided a sense of movement, and the subject matter was so surreal, that even without the influence of a hallucinogenic, Sara felt as if she could walk right into the picture.

Scraping away the last strip of white between the greenhouses and the house took some work. The paint coverage was thicker there, as if having been layered rather than the quick single-coat cover afforded the rest of the wall. With the care of an archeologist unearthing a new dinosaur, she gently worked away the paint. A humanoid creature—and she had no doubt it was another monster—began to emerge. This one was brown and wrinkled. Round, gray spots which she supposed were eyes, hovered above a drape of flesh pulled up just slightly in the midline to expose a set of long incisors. Its head was smooth, like the lake monster's, but the rest of its body was folds of flesh with—not webbed digits—but skinny, elongated ones with claws of equal length. Sara shuddered, part in revulsion and part in excitement because it, too, had been done later, by the same artist who'd painted the lake monster. The body shapes and styles were similar, as was the heavy-handed paint application.

Were there more creatures hiding there, beneath a quick and cheap cover-up?

More. More had to be uncovered. She worked frantically. Her shoulder and biceps burned, but it didn't matter. She hadn't eaten, but that didn't matter, either. She had to uncover the entire wall. She had to know the secrets of The Children of Demeter. A wall of green bordered the lower edge of the mural. She followed it, crawling on her left hand and knees and working the scraper with her right. When she reached the far corner, she headed back up toward the caves where Roy had described an altar and time-bending sex. She'd experienced the same—apparently—only her situation was much worse, in that the sex was also mind-breaking. She remembered nothing.

The artist's depiction of the first two caves was that of tan, rounded breasts. Spilling forth from the nippled entrances was not milk but honey—thick, golden, and nourishing. Sara remembered how Roy said the first few caves held fermenting fruits and honey. It was the large one, closer to the crater wall, where he and Merry had worshipped in the old ways.

Before she could uncover it, the doorbell rang. She jumped and dropped the scraper. Her hand cramped into an immovable claw.

"Shit! Just a minute!" she called out. *Please don't let it be Stephanie. I'm not ready for so much optimism.*

Whoever it was had the patience of a saint, because they did not ring or knock again. The cramp dissipated reluctantly, and her knees creaked in protest as she stood fully upright. By the time she made it to the door, she realized there was no one waiting for her. Clearly, it had been a delivery.

I swear to all that is holy, if Shirley sent me one more thing of Phil's, I will take a video of myself destroying it and send it back to her.

There was no package. Instead, on the porch at her feet, sat what looked to be a photo album with a manila envelope lying on top of it. There was no writing on the envelope, nothing with her name or address on it. She looked around and craned to see beyond the stone arch where cars parked but saw no one. Sara took the book and envelope, shut, and locked the door.

The book wasn't a photo album at all but a ledger of some sort. Headings titled *First Fruits*, *Harvest*, *Cross-Over*, and *Resurrection* seemed to be marking chapters or segments of the book. Beneath the headings were lists of names. Each name was followed by a date and then either the number one or two. If the number was a one, it was further classified with the letter M or F. No such addition had been made to the number twos. She put the album down and opened the envelope.

Several black and white photographs spilled out onto her lap—pictures of the commune in its heyday. She leafed through them, her heart pounding and hands shaking. Here she was, looking at the commune's members—the worshippers of Demeter. Many photos depicted people topless or completely naked. In several pictures, she found pregnant women. In almost every photo, at least one of the women looked so pregnant she must have been a month overdue. Even in black and white, Sara could see skin straining to hold back a womb ready to burst. *Like the fruits on the orchard trees in the painting.*

Who'd left these for her? Stephanie? *Julie. It had to be Julie.* She said she would look through their storage and see what she could find. The ledger was probably something kept by the newspaper—maybe from a journalist who followed the cult, keeping track of something. Sara decided she should call Julie, thank her, and see if she had any knowledge of the written record.

She carried her prizes upstairs to her room. Fishing out her cell phone and plugging it in, she searched for the card Jeff gave her with the temporary passwords for logging onto the new satellite WiFi he'd installed. When her long dead phone finally powered up, the voicemail notification beeped.

Andrea. Or maybe Reggie or Stu. Her throat tightened a bit. She didn't bother with the password; she knew her voicemail would play at least. If she had to call someone back, had to eat crow and try to apologize, she would worry about the login then. She took a breath and hit play.

"Hi Sara, this is Dr. Paulson. I got your labs and biopsy results back earlier than expected, so I wanted to call you right away. Everything is normal. Your hormone levels are premenopausal, and the tissue from your biopsy is consistent with normal menses. You were just having a period! No cancer. I can't explain the long absence of your period, but its back now, for better or worse." She laughed a short chuckle then stopped. "But, seriously, I know you said you were told you could never conceive, but these labs and this biopsy prove otherwise. I realize your husband died recently, but if you happen to end up in a new relationship, I would strongly recommend some form of contraception, unless you want to have a baby at forty-six! Give me a call if you have any questions. Bye, now."

Chapter 19

Sara waited for the air to return to her lungs. The phone hung loose in her fist. Her stomach turned, and she thought she might throw up.

You're not pregnant. It's too early to even consider it. It's just an empty stomach and way too much right now. Stop panicking. Just breathe.

The nausea passed and oxygen found its way back to her brain. She found the login card in her purse and used it to return to the world online and search for Julie's number. Realizing it was Sunday and no one would be at the newspaper, she decided to get some food instead. At the bottom of the stairs, sat Phil's urn. The symbol she'd scratched on it glinted in the afternoon sun shining through the front door's glass pane.

She plopped down on the last step and picked up the vessel, turning it in her hands slowly, like the rotation of the earth through the years she'd spent with him. There'd been good times, of course. Upon deeper consideration, those times had been on the vacations *he* chose or doing the activities *he* liked to do. She remembered listening to his almost lecture-like tutorials on gourmet cooking or mountain biking. His insistence that she find interest in these things, too, or else it meant she didn't love him. She'd tried. She had, but thinking back, had he ever done the same for her? Had he ever taken her traveling or sightseeing? Had he shown interest in her landscaping plans?

"God, you were such a selfish bastard," she said to the urn. "So, what happened, Phil? Did I not worship you enough? Did my intellect and my interests separate from yours turn out to be too much?"

She saw the text exchanges between Phil and Marie in her head. She'd read them so many times. His sweetness that he'd never shared with Sara, Marie's flirtations that did not garner an "K, sounds good" from him. Their plans for a medical conference—the kind to which he'd never invited his wife. She didn't know the man in those texts. The sweet, kind man, who'd showered attention on a woman who'd done nothing for him except stroke his ego for a month or two—attention he'd never showered on his wife.

"Remember when I lost the baby, Phil? How I laid on the bed in pain and bleeding, and you sat in the corner staring ahead like a deer in the headlights? Did you comfort me? So, you know what? Fuck your little whore. I hope she's dying in agony, too. And you're dead. You're not there for her, either. That's exactly what you both deserve."

Her tears were coming heavy, and the air once again clawed to escape her chest, leaving her aching and hollow. She'd wanted that baby so much. Having been abandoned by her own mother as a baby, she'd wanted the chance to prove she would be better. She would be the parent her adopted mother and father had been. It had meant everything to her to give her child the legacy she'd never had. But Phil watched it go as if it meant nothing. Marie had her own kids. Was he seriously considering her as a partner? He had to have known what that would do to Sara when or if she'd found out.

She carried the urn out the front door and to the well.

"Demeter can have you," she said, and threw it as hard as she could into the hole. "And don't you dare come back!"

Her stomach growled in agreement. On her way back inside via the side door leading into the kitchen, she noticed the ivy sprouts coming up again. More this time, and they were longer. She made a mental note to come out with her phone after dinner and document the changes. It was the only way to ensure belief.

She didn't remember, though. After a dinner of microwaved canned stew and a slice of buttered bread, she retired to the clawfoot tub with a glass of wine and spent the evening deleting her late ex-husband's existence from her phone and catching up on social media.

The hot water cooled, and she dragged herself out. Aching muscles and emotional exhaustion clung to her like a fat suit. She trudged to the sink, towel dried her hair, and began working the comb through it. Her eyes wandered to the window where, the night before, she'd done something unimaginable and lost her best friend. She replayed all her memories before the blackout that remained her only defense for her actions.

Eyelids, heavy with grief and confusion, fell. She squeezed them tight. When she opened them, she looked right into the mirror in front of her. Before she could focus on her own face, someone in the background of the mirror image caught her attention. Only a split second, a flash, but enough for Sara to be sure she saw it.

"Hey!" She took off after it, her towel barely holding on as she sprinted down the stairs. She heard the door in the kitchen open and shut. She tore through the living room and out the side door without thinking. The towel gave up on the porch and dropped to cover her bare feet.

Roy Kumpula stood in her side yard staring into the well. When he looked up and saw her, he quickly shaded his eyes with the brim of his cap and looked back into the abyss.

Sara grabbed her towel and covered herself. "What were you doing in my house? You were spying on me taking a bath? I'm calling the cops!"

"Wasn't me in your house, but I believe you when you say somebody was." He kept his head down.

"Get. Off. My. Property. Now!" she screamed at the top of her lungs. "Get out of my life!"

She slammed the door. Somewhere in her purse, she had a bottle of Xanax that Dr. Templeton had given her after Phil's accident. If she took two, she'd sleep. But first, she locked every door and window in the place.

"Might as well wash it down with the rest of the wine," she said, grabbing the bottle and heading up to bed.

Even connected to the WiFi, the only music that would play were the sounds of 1960's California. She drifted off to sleep to Brian Wilson's *In My Room*, feeling as safe and likely as drugged as he.

Phil came to her. He brushed the hair from her face the way he did when he was feeling romantic, the way he did when they were so much younger. God, it felt good. He ran his hand down her arm. She felt him examine the bandage. He peeled it off gently. She winced when the gauze pulled at a scab. The rough skin of his thumb ran over it so lightly, it could have been his breath. Maybe it was. It was her dream, after all. If she wanted him to be kneeling at her bedside about to kiss away her pain, she could have that.

Grave dirt fell from him, sprinkling her arm, her sheets, her wound. She brushed it away with her other hand. He'd come back from the dead for her, clawed his way up from the depths of the earth for her. *Phil was cremated. There is no grave.* But if it wasn't grave dirt, then what was it? Her eyes remained closed as she emerged slowly from sleep, she reached out to him, feeling for his body. She couldn't open her eyes, not if he was there in his mangled, broken form. She didn't want to see that again. Never. If it were post-crash Phil, then it was probably broken glass falling on her and not grave dirt at all.

Open your eyes and look. Just open your eyes. Don't touch him.

No. Keeping her eyes closed and staying under the covers kept her safe. A childish belief, perhaps, but in the dark and alone, even grown-ups believed. She reached out with her good hand and touched bare flesh. It was thick, like she expected an elephant's skin would feel. Intact chest, not caved in and lacerated from the windshield. She reached higher, her fingers rolling over a topography of wrinkles she did not know. The chin did not have the piece of steering wheel that she was told had been lodged in its base. Just beyond the chin, though, her fingers touched teeth. Two long, sharp-edged teeth.

The monster from the mural. It wasn't a dream; it was a nightmare. She *had* to open her eyes. She needed to wake up. It was the only way to make it go away. Obeying her fight or flight response, she looked. Darkness filled the room. At first, she saw nothing, but as she grew accustomed to the night, an outline emerged of a creature with moonlight glinting off its teeth. Sara screamed.

It ran. Sara didn't run after it. Instead, she waited in bed, under the covers, until she heard the door and understood it wasn't the door to outside. It was the one in the corner of the kitchen—the one she didn't have the key for—the one that led to a basement with dirt walls and large tunnels. She got up, tiptoed through the darkness to her own door, which she shut and locked. The Xanax hadn't approved of this awakening. It strongly suggested she go back to sleep immediately and worry about what she may *or may not have* seen later.

A nightmare brought on by booze and benzos. That's all. Once her heart slowed, she fell back asleep.

Chapter 20

Monday morning came as Mondays do—unwanted and too soon. Her head hurt. She rolled out of bed and sat on her bedroom floor. Mama Cass sang *Dream a Little Dream of Me,* and Sara vaguely recalled her own strange dream. One where Phil had come back from the dead and then turned into the newest monster from the mural—the one that looked like one of those naked mole rats that always seemed to be on the nature shows.

She stood up and turned to make up the bed. Dirt marred her sheets. Someone or something *had* been in her bedroom while she slept. Goosebumps rolled up her arms and converged on the back of her neck. She shivered. Not cold but bothered—bothered because there were only two explanations for the evidence. First and least likely, she had indeed been visited by some mutant cross between a human and a mole or second, her neighbor had somehow gotten into her home and dropped some field dirt onto her bed as he attempted to assault her.

You're forgetting the most likely explanation—You've lost your mind. You're sleepwalking and/or having blackouts where you fornicate with kids young enough to be your own child, or go digging in the dirt and then crawl back in to bed.

She checked the bottom of her feet—clean. The door to her room was still locked. She vaguely remembered locking it when she'd gone back to bed after her dream. So, it had been Roy. The man was relentless. As she showered, she considered every interaction she had with him. His behavior toward her swung between creepy and paternalistic, while the man who Reggie and Stu interviewed seemed thoughtful and introspective. *But also hiding something.* Yes, he wasn't telling the truth or at least not the *entire* truth. As a sociologist, she prided herself on noting behavior patterns that implied deceit. *You missed a big one with Phil, though, didn't you? Maybe you're not such a hotshot after all.*

Her fully charged cellphone played hits of the '60's while she looked up the number and called *The Citizen*. Julie came to the phone before the on-hold recording could tell her what Al's Drills and Pills had to offer for their weekly sale.

"Hi, Sara! So good to hear from you. I wondered when I might get to talk to you again."

"Hey there. Listen, someone left a package of pictures and what looks like a record book of some sort on my doorstep yesterday. The pics were of people from the Demeter clan and a ledger that, I have to say, I cannot exactly decipher. I was thinking maybe it was you or someone from the paper?"

"Oh. Really? I'd love to see them. But to answer your question, no. No one here sent them. But, boy, that makes me want to head to the storage area and dig up some stuff. You free this afternoon?"

"I can be, for sure."

"Well, come on down. I'll get started as soon as I can. Give me a heads-up when you're on your way so I can be here to meet you. Bring the photos and ledger."

"Absolutely, I'd love to hear your take on them."

"No problem. I'm excited to be a part of your research."

"I'll be sure to acknowledge you if the book ever sees the light of day. See you later."

Sara hung up. So, if it wasn't Julie, it must have been Stephanie. She found her real estate agent and first Wisconsin friend in her contacts then dialed.

"Hi. This is Stephanie Pierce. It's a great day in West Burma! How can I help you?"

"Stephanie, it's Sara. Hey, so I called because I was wondering if you might have dropped off some old pictures of The Children of Demeter clan and some kind of ledger, maybe something they kept? Someone left it on my doorstep. I called Julie; she didn't know anything about it."

"Really? No, I didn't but I would love to see them. What a mystery! What are you doing right now?"

"Uh, I, uh, well, nothing, actually. I was going to meet up with Julie this afternoon, but other than that, I'm free." She thought longingly of the wall mural in the living room, but she had plenty of time before the crew arrived and, frankly, she'd love to hear Stephanie's thoughts on the ledger. Maybe, if she played her cards right, Stephanie would grant access to her grandparents, too.

"Slims? In, say, an hour? I'm showing a house in about five minutes, but after that I'm free."

"Slim's it is."

Sara was ready, having bathed last night. She pulled her hair up into a ponytail and threw on some decent looking clothes. It was too hot to put on makeup. Besides, who did she have to impress? She decided to kill some time with a walk around the property.

Ivy vines crawled up the posts placed in the ground forty years before. Sara bent down and petted them.

"Grow, little ones. Grow up big and lush and strong. Roy has no business snooping on us." The mushrooms at the greenhouse had returned, larger and fuller than before. Their stems were long and thin, but their caps were tucked close to their middles. She smiled. Their growth was pleasing.

At the sides of the house, tiny, baby vines clung to their dead progenitors. Before November's chill took them away, they'd reach the windows. The place was coming back to life along with Sara. She smiled, happy with their collective progress.

"All hail the Goddess," Sara told the ground.

She checked the well, shining the light from her phone into the murky depths, but she couldn't see the bottom. It didn't matter. Phil was down there, trapped in his urn. Cremated. In ashes. *He didn't come back last night; he didn't visit my bed.* And that was all she needed to know.

The backyard was a still life. No wind ruffled the lake's surface, no monster visited from the depths. She watched for some time before giving up. The muck between the lake and the caves was probably three hundred feet at least. She tried a step or two into it, but it sucked at her shoes and she retreated.

The drive to Slim's was silent. Sara didn't think she could take one more minute of tunes from long-dead or retired singers.

Stephanie sat at a booth right in the front. She stood and waved calling Sara's name. Sara hurried over, not appreciating the sudden looks from all the diners. She sat down quickly and smiled.

"So good to see a friendly face," Sara said.

"Who hasn't been friendly to you?" Stephanie asked maternally.

"Well, Roy Kumpula for one. I suppose you could say he has been *overly* friendly...in a menacing way." She wasn't about to get into the problem with Andrea, because how could she even begin to explain that?

"Sara, you know, as a realtor, I shouldn't speak poorly of your neighbors. But as your friend, I'm telling you that man is trouble. I've always held a firm belief that he had something to do with the commune's disappearance."

Sara sat up straighter and leaned over the table. "How?" She'd lowered her voice.

"He had a thing for one of the clan members. I don't know. Whatever he did, I suppose he thought he was saving her."

"So, does that make him bad?" Sara remembered the story of Merry that Roy had told during his interview with Reggie and Stu.

"He had no business interfering with something he didn't understand. He made judgements from an outsider's perspective, and it may have cost them all their lives." Their server—Gail, again—came by and took their orders.

Sara tried to get Stephanie back to the story. "I feel like you know something you're not telling me, Stephanie. I wish you would, though. It would really help me write this book."

"I was just a kid, Sara. It's all just conjecture on my part. But I can tell you this—the guy is always creeping around the property. He's scared away more than a few previous owners. Whatever he tells you, take it with a grain of salt." She winked. "By that, I mean throw it over your shoulder and walk away."

Stephanie was definitely keeping something from her. But why? *Because she's afraid it will scare you off, duh. You think she wants to have to try to sell that place again? Well, she isn't going to scare me off. I like the house, and it's coming along. With the vines regrowing and the mural on the wall, it's a nice little place. Just needs to be fumigated for mutants, is all.* She snorted a little. Stephanie took it as a belated reaction to her salt joke.

"Eh, he's a silly old man. Don't even worry about him. Now, let's see these pictures."

Sara pulled them out of the ledger she'd carried in and handed the stack to Stephanie. She studied the woman's reaction. Stephanie looked each one over before putting it in the back of the stack. She stopped at one with a group of children in it. They played together, or maybe danced in a ring, all holding hands. Some as young as two or three and others in their early teens. Stephanie laid it to the side facedown. She looked at the last two. She pointed to a girl of about seventeen or eighteen in the last picture.

"This is Merry. The one Roy had a thing for." She handed the stack back to Sara who stared hard at the woman in the photo. Something seemed familiar about her, as if she'd known the woman before—in another life perhaps. Or maybe it was because she'd heard Roy talk about her, so the girl was more real than the rest. Still, though, her eyes and nose...

"Do you mind if I keep this one for a day or two?" Stephanie's question interrupted her thoughts. "There are some kids here I think I recognize. I'd like to show my grandparents, get their opinions."

"Oh sure! That would be great, actually." The idea of having names with faces was fantastic. A section of pictures would make the book even better.

"Wonderful. I'll bring it back to you as soon as I get a chance to talk to them." She shoved the photo in her purse just as their lunch arrived.

Chapter 21

Julie waited with a Cheshire cat grin on her face as Sara arrived at the office.

"I hit the jackpot. Did you bring your pictures? I found a bunch, too! Come on downstairs."

Sara followed her to the basement of the building, which was filled with warehouse type shelves covered in plastic tub totes labeled with years. Julie had pulled down five totes from the years '68-73. Sara glanced inside the boxes as they walked by to see manila envelopes carefully stacked inside. At the table in the corner, a pile of photos waited.

"Most of these pictures were taken at the farmer's market, but it looks like some of them were sent in as well."

Sara shuffled through many pictures of various clan members who stood proudly beside a table filled with produce. She stopped at one featuring a quite pregnant Merry. In fact, impossibly larger than any pregnant woman Sara had ever seen. She turned the picture over to check for dates on the back. In a neat cursive hand, someone had scrawled 8/9/73, RK036, Children of Demeter member Merry Dai.

"She looks like she had a tumor not a baby in there," Sara said. The woman in the picture smiled directly into the camera, her eyes bright and twinkling. Not a fake smile, not one put on at the urging of the photographer, but one that said Merry knew and liked the photographer.

"A lot of them look that way in these pics. Guess they grew their babies as big as their fruit."

Sara pulled her pictures out of the ledger. She spread them out in front of Julie. Julie picked them up and scanned them one at a time. She nodded at a few and laid those ones out separate. Then she leaned over the pile in front of Sara and sorted them, picking out matching faces, like that memory game toddlers liked to play. By the time Julie finished, she had matched all of Sara's photos to her own.

"We can probably identify most of the people in these pictures by process of elimination." She jumped up and grabbed a notebook. The two women worked together all afternoon, reading the names on the backs of pictures from the paper and matching them to those in Sara's until they'd named most of the women and all but three of the men.

"Over five years, almost every one of these women were tumor pregnant once and regular pregnant at least once, if not more than once." Sara observed.

Julie nodded.

"I know. It's strange. Do you think maybe there was a preponderance of twins or triplets?" Julie asked then chewed on the clicker of her pen.

"Do you have any pictures of kids?" Sara asked, wishing she hadn't given Stephanie her one and only clear picture of older children. She'd only casually glanced at it, not feeling it was as important as those of the adults.

"Oh yeah! In fact, I have the cutest one of Roger when he was a little boy with his little girlfriend from Demeter. It's so cute." She rummaged through another envelope they hadn't even opened yet. "These pictures were taken by a newspaper employee and not sent in, so they're kept separate," she explained needlessly.

The picture of Roger and his "girlfriend," both around seven or eight years old, was indeed cute. The little girl with cotton-colored hair flying wild in the breeze was topless and wearing dhoti-type shorts. Her toothy grin was exuberant. She reminded Sara of Pippi Longstocking from her favorite childhood stories.

"Who is this girl?" she asked Julie.

"I don't know. Roger can't remember her name."

"Oh, shoot. Ok. Are there any other pictures of kids? Like groups that we could check for twins or look-alikes?"

"Uh, let's see," Julie looked through the last envelope. "No, no groups of kids. A lot of these pictures have one or two in them but not enough together in the same to say there are twins."

"And no women holding more than one at a time, either. So much for that theory," Sara sighed.

"Did you see this one, though?" Julie held one out for Sara to see. "It's your neighbor, Roy Kumpula! See, the back of this one has the caption that ran with it.

Indeed, it was Roy and Merry, but in that picture, she wasn't pregnant. In it, she held an apple out, and he had just grabbed it. His fingers touched hers. They both smiled at the photographer. The caption on the back read, "Local boy and soldier, Roy Kumpula, home from Vietnam, stops by The Children of Demeter booth for a healthy snack."

"I think they were sweet on each other," Julie said. "Too cute. Such a lovely old man. He'd do absolutely anything for you. Roger helps out a lot on his farm. Roy has no kids or family. Sometimes I think Roger would be thrilled if Roy left it all to him. Me, on the other hand…" Julie blew her bangs up with a well-aimed burst of air. "It's a little more work than I'd like to get into. But Roy is just wonderful, he really is. Have you met him yet?"

The kind words about Roy caught her off guard. Stephanie had nothing nice to say about him, yet Julie seemed to think the world of the man. "No, not really. I mean we've said hello, but that's about it."

"Well, Roy is just about a jack of all trades. He's always offering to lend whatever kind of hand is needed. And he's a great photographer. Half of these pictures are his." She grabbed one up from the neatly organized stacks and turned it over. "See? RK023. Roy Kumpula. We number all the ones he took and sent to us. I bet that's where those ones of yours came from. He probably stopped by to share them with you, knowing what you're up to and all."

"Roy took these pictures?" Sara looked through the stack to the one of pregnant Merry flirting with the photographer and turned it over just to be sure. RK036.

He said he never saw her again after their stint in the cave, yet this is clearly toward the end of their stay at Demeter House. I think I need to have a chat with Mr. Kumpula.

"Uh huh. Quite talented." Julie took the picture of Merry from Sara's hand. "You know, this could be you as a teenager. Do you have any children, Sara?"

A lump rose into Sara's throat and threatened to close off her trachea. The internal self-strangulation caused hot tears to form in the corner of her eyes. She shook her head no. Julie took her hand.

"Oh, I am so sorry. I did not mean to hit a nerve. Really, I'm so stupid sometimes, I ask stupid questions. Why don't we have a look at that ledger book? See if it can't help us make sense of things?"

Sara sniffled and nodded. She took the book out, interested in looking again after going through all the pictures. She remembered some of the names from the lists in the ledger.

Julie slid her chair over beside Sara and opened the book on the table in front of them. She scanned the first page then the second without a word. Sara didn't say anything when Julie turned the pages at her pace without asking Sara if she was through looking. When she'd gone through all the entries, she returned to the beginning and tapped the first name, Summer Raye. She ran a finger across the page to the date and the number two.

"This is a pregnancy record, I think," Julie said sitting up straighter in her chair. "Look at the dates and compare to the pregnant girls in the pictures." She held up Summer's pregnant picture as an example. The dates were close. She grabbed another named Sunny Dew and compared. In every picture of what Sara and she had started to refer to as the tumor babies, the dates matched and all were marked with a two.

"If the two means twins," Sara pondered, "Then, first of all, there was something in the water up here. Secondly, where did the babies go?"

"Maybe they shared childrearing, so we only see a woman holding one baby because another woman has the other, you know?"

"Yeah, makes sense," Sara tapped the blank space beside the number twos where the ones had an M or F added. Julie picked up on her thoughts.

"Weird that they only note the gender for the single babies, but never with the twins. I don't know, it's still a lot of twins, if that's what it means."

"You know, there are tribes in Africa with a crazy high rate of twinning, I wonder if this clan was somehow predisposed as well. I need to look up if there is genetic link to genders as well. Like, what if the twins were always two boys or two girls, so they didn't bother to mark it?" There was a lot to think about. "Julie, can I get a cell phone pic of the photo of Roger and his little girlfriend? And all the ones with kids in them? I lent a pic to Stephanie to show her grandparents of a bunch of kids. I'm gonna see if I can get that back."

"Oh, sure, but don't tell Roger I showed it to you. He doesn't like me looking at all this stuff. Says the whole Demeter thing is nothing but a hoax that put West Burma unnecessarily in the national spotlight and on all the freak websites.

He hates it when paranormal investigators show up in town and start asking questions. Most of the town does, actually. They'd all like to forget it. That's why everyone is talking about you and what it is you're really up to. They don't understand that you're a real scientist." She smiled reassuringly. "But I get it. And I get the needing some alone time, too. I heard about your husband."

"Oh great. Well, good. I'm glad that's out in the open," Sara grumbled. She might have to have a talk with Stephanie about privacy. Also, she needed to get out of there before Julie started asking stupid questions again. "I'm gonna snap those pics now and head out. Do you know where Stephanie's grandparent's live? I think I might stop by and see if that picture is there."

Julie gave her directions and apologized again for bringing up painful subjects. "Here." Julie stuffed all the pictures into one envelope and folded up the notebook pages where they'd kept notes. "You take all this for your research. I think you're on to something about the twinning. I'll put everything away, and Roger won't even need to know we got into all this today. But you better get out of here before he gets back." She grinned, but Sara saw it quiver. There was a little worry there, too. What would Roger say if he did find out they'd been looking at this stuff? Wasn't he supposed to help her, anyway? Why was he dragging his feet? Julie clearly didn't know, or else she would have never helped Sara. In fact, Sara doubted Julie ever purposefully disobeyed her husband. She also bet, if Julie did, there was hell to pay.

Chapter 22

No one was home at the Pierce's or Kumpula farm, so Sara went back to Demeter House. She felt closer to the clan there, and she could think about all of the new information more clearly. The vines filled in somewhat and had started their climb up the poles on the property's border—as if they sprouted from magical beans, so fast they grew.

"Good," Sara announced to the empty house. "Maybe Roy will get the hint."

Her stomach reminded her that she hadn't eaten since brunch with Stephanie. Soup was the answer to the problem. Soup and grilled cheese. She hummed Jefferson Airplane as she warmed up the can of cheese broccoli soup and toasted the provolone filled sandwich.

She absently flipped through the ledger. There was something there, something right under her nose, yet, she couldn't figure it out. Pages of names, dates, and either a one or a two. Pregnancy ledger. Julie was right, but why, and who cared? If the number two meant twins, then it would seem every female member had at least one set of twins during the time the ledger recorded. Stephanie had the picture of utmost importance.

Don't you think, if there had been a couple sets of look-alike kids in that pic, you would have noticed? True, but at the time, she'd been more interested in the adults.

She flipped to the last page of notes. *Harvest.* The last person listed with a two was Merry Dai. The date listed stopped Sara's heart: September 16, 1973. The date the doctor bestowed upon her as her probable birthdate when she was first discovered abandoned in a mall.

It's a coincidence. These women were prolific breeders, clearly. The cult worshipped a fertility goddess. Of course there would be babies born around your birthdate, which, by the way, is only a guesstimate at best.

A soft thud, followed by a rattle from the corner door leading to the basement, brought her out of her musing. She knocked the chair over in her rush to the door. This time it opened without issue, so she flew down the steps after whatever had been spying on her. Rounding the corner to the room with holes in the dirt walls, she was just in time to see the crumbles of dirt hit the floor from a tunnel in the far wall where an empty shelf had been removed and still neatly leaned against the wall beneath it.

Sara put her hands on her hips. It was getting ridiculous. Either she was really and truly insane or some*thing* was spying on her.

She had an idea.

"Ugh," she groaned out loud—probably louder than necessary—and went back upstairs, taking the steps with heavier footfalls than needed.

About a bowlful of soup remained in the pan and almost half a sandwich sat on her plate. She refilled her bowl and carried the dinner downstairs and to the most recently used escape tunnel. Grabbing a bottle of mead, she plopped down onto the pile of shawls and blankets and waited. And waited.

The thick, sweet drink made her thoughts heavy. Ideas of monsters infesting her home trudged through her honeyed brain. Circling around a center of doubt, they danced among the bare-breasted women of Demeter's Children, changing with each rotation from Lake Monster and Mole Creature to Phil and Marie to Merry and Roy. The hypnotic sequence lulled her to sleep and the empty bottle rolled from her hand.

Sara woke with a startle and a neck spasm that made her gasp. It took her eyes a moment to adjust to the low light of the root cellar. Her consciousness took slightly longer to adjust to her location. Ah, yes, she'd fallen asleep waiting for a monster to be lured to the opening of its tunnel by the scent of broccoli cheese soup and half of a cold grilled cheese sandwich. Being the ever-vigilant scientist, she was, she'd then drank herself into a stupor.

It's not like you actually thought a mole-person was really going to come crawling out to have some soup and a sandwich while you watched like a kid at the zoo. Andrea's right, you need some serious help.

"Okay, dumb idea," she announced to the empty room, and walked over to the tunnel to collect the food and dishes.

Neither were there.

"What the hell?" She leaned deeper inside, but there were no dishes anywhere. Knowing it was a futile effort, she still walked around the room to check every other hole in the dirt walls. Nothing. *This is crazy. I must have drunk way more than I thought, got frustrated, and took the stuff back upstairs.*

"Right, and then came back downstairs to grab a nap on old musty blankets?" She rolled her eyes at her own thoughts.

It was late. She was surprised it wasn't dark already. Maybe it was time to do the last of the mural excavating before bed. Shuffling back upstairs, she couldn't help but notice all the dirt on the stairs. *There ya go, I carried the stuff up earlier and got a bunch of dirt on the steps.*

"I guess you ate it all before you brought it up, too," she snapped back when she saw the empty bowl and plate sitting on the counter by the sink. Her soup bowl, which was also empty, sat on the kitchen table by the pictures, which she could have sworn she'd left scattered out but were now in one neat pile. Gritty dirt lay scattered on the kitchen floor.

The constant inner battle between sanity and madness exhausted her. If it was true the heart only had so many beats per lifetime, then the house, this situation, would use hers up in mere weeks. *I'll be dead by Thanksgiving.* At that point, she wasn't sure it was a bad thing, either.

A random electronic notification echoed from the living room—voicemail. Leaving the mystery behind, she padded to the edge of the linoleum and brushed her feet off with her hand one at a time before stepping on to the paper-thin carpet. The cell phone's battery was at 10% and insisted the time was 5:30 AM, which was absurd. She'd gone to the basement last night around 6:00 pm, and there was just no way she'd been asleep for nearly eleven hours. Andrea's voice sounded tentative and practiced when Sara hit the play button on her voicemail.

"Hello, Sara. I wanted to touch base with you before the fifteenth. Bill and I discussed some things, and we decided to only bring two students a piece. I think more than that might be overwhelming for you. No, I did not tell Bill anything about what happened, if you're wondering. As for what did happen, Reggie and Stu aren't even sure. I'm giving you the benefit of the doubt, Sara. Phil's death, your isolation in that town, and all the madness associated with the house has screwed up your head. The boys admitted to smoking some pot with you, and I suppose it could have been laced with something. Who knows? Just try to get yourself together before we get there, and I'll do my best not to behave as if I want to strangle you. Oh, and can you get the area by the greenhouses cleared up? I'm going to have the University get a couple new ones put up before we get there. They'll tear the old ones down, if you can just clear a space and some of the glass away. See you in exactly twelve days."

Sara deleted the recording and tossed the phone on the couch.

"Well, I sure hope I can find the time to clean up around the greenhouses, what with all the time it might take to get myself together, Queen An."

It was time for the mural. She had all day, really. The mural had to come first. Then she would deal with the pictures, and Roy, and the monsters, and don't forget, Andrea's ridiculous demands. But there would be no sleep until the rest of the secrets of Demeter's Children had been unearthed.

Chapter 23

By noon, the last and most important cave had been excavated from the wall. In the drawing, as opposed to real life, the cave was significantly larger than the rest. It hosted the symbol from the baluster like a TV antenna and spilled forth all sorts of life in its many forms like a cornucopia. On top of the various flora and fauna sat a thin, pale, devil-like creature. The newest creature appeared smaller than the lake monster or the mole-person—child-sized, with white, sightless eyes and elongated, pointed ears.

"Who painted you?" Sara asked, touching the thick layer of cadaverous gray making up the creature. "And when?"

When the cave child gave no answer, she continued to search beneath the paint.

The end of the backyard beyond the lake coincided with the uppermost portion of the living room wall. Where, in reality, a concave cliff rose and protectively embraced the land where the Demeter House stood. In the mural, they were cupped hands, presumably of the mother goddess.

"It's beautiful," Sara murmured. The maternal hands brought a sudden womb-like comfort to the room, and she felt protected and at peace.

She was so close to seeing the art in its completed form. All that remained was the bit of the side yard that covered the well. She went to work.

Sometime during the final rally of paint scraping, the air conditioners in the house stopped running. Sweat dripped down her face, into her eyes. She swiped at it with the back of her forearm. Finally, when the cruel heat slowed her progress, she stripped down to her underwear.

What Sara originally anticipated to be nothing more than swirls of green and maybe a glowing or brightly colored disc in the center of the side yard, turned into the only scene in the entire mural to depict people. Women, in various stages of pregnancy, danced in a ring around—not a colorful slab—but a black hole. The scene reminded Sara of Matisse's *The Dance,* and she suspected the artist was channeling Matisse when they painted it. The women leaned and flowed around the well. The only difference was, where Matisse's dancers pranced around on green earth, Demeter's children trod on red.

The last human link in the circle was all that she had left to uncover. Then, and only then, would she allow herself food and drink and a shower. Her mouth was cotton, but excitement trumped thirst. Triumph in task completion cured dehydration. She ignored the blisters on her fingers where the scraper pressed against them. The sweat made it difficult to keep a good hold, so she had to push harder and hold tighter. Her biceps screamed and her deltoid threatened to freeze, but she had to finish.

The head was not at the level of the others. Brow furrowed, lips pressed tight; Sara worked lower. There couldn't be a body missing here. A break in the moving ring? It made no sense. But then a head, a golden blond mane of hair, appeared beneath her scraper. The head appeared at waist-level of the other dancers. She squatted. Squatted and—oh, god—gave birth.

It was done. The wall, with it's fifty-year-old mural, completely revealed. Sara stared at the frenzied scene. It wasn't a dance, not a ring of revelers at all. The group of women swayed back and forth to encourage the laboring woman. Blood poured from her womb and spilled into the grass around the well. Beneath the new mother, on the reddened ground between her and the well, two babies lay side by side. One with eyes open and arms outstretched, all pink and rosy-cheeked. The other baby dusky, eyes closed, and marked with the symbol Sara decided stood for Demeter on its chest.

Beneath Demeter's child, the trail of blood led directly to the well, while the happy little twin nested in its own pool which led nowhere else.

"That child belongs to the earth," Sara said, and shook the thought away. Where had that come from? Clearly, it was a stillborn. Perhaps the scene depicted more of a funeral than a celebration of birth? "No. The Goddess has laid claim by the mark upon her flesh. The babe, like Persephone, is the child of Demeter. She must be placed within the womb of the earth mother."

Sara touched the chosen one. A jolt of electricity traveled through her fingers and buzzed within the denuded skin of her own birthmark. She scratched at it absentmindedly. Water. *I need water now.* She was thirsty.

At the sink, where she guzzled glass after glass of cool tap water, Sara looked out at the lake. A gentle breeze rippled the surface, causing small waves to curl like a finger beckoning her to come, to submerge her hot, sweaty body within its cooling arms. She put the glass down and followed the water's command. *Come.*

The first step into the lake sent a rush of goosebumps up her body like dominoes defying gravity. She shook them off and continued. The silt at the bottom was as smooth as the silk tops of corn growing in her neighbor's field. Mud oozed between her toes, sucking them as a lover might do. Her sex swelled and lurched towards the aquatic foreplay. Her knees buckled, bringing the water level to her navel. She shivered with anticipation before pushing off the bottom and embracing the lake with her full body.

The cool, wetness enveloped her, washing away the day's sweat and dirt. Her bandage was water-logged and she tore it off, tossing the soggy ball of gauze to the shore. The lake licked her wound and offered to do the same to her nethers, should she take off her underwear. She obliged, throwing them as well. Cold water had stiffened her nipples and heightened their sensitivity. Her breaths grew ragged with each scissor kick that pulled a current across her clitoris. She panted and worked her legs until she threw her head back in ecstasy and called out praises to the goddess.

Suddenly something grabbed her leg and yanked her down. She had a second to gasp a breath before she was under and sinking fast. The surface receded in her murky vision. Sara kicked. Nails dug into her flesh. She kicked again and again and again, finding a solid target more times than not. With each contact, the grip loosened, and she slipped more of her leg away. Her arms swept madly, pulling herself upward to the surface. She broke through once and exchanged the oxygen-depleted air for fresh before the thing had her again, this time around her waist. Clawed feet climbed up her legs, gouging wounds in her flesh. She squirmed and wriggled.

She reached down with her hand and swiped at the smooth dome of the thing's head. Her attacker writhed as she sliced into its soft, amphibious skin with her fingernails. The creature tried to pull its head away while holding onto her. She kicked and it kicked back. Her legs were hot with blood. Sara attacked the head of the monster. Skin slid away easily allowing her fingers to sink deeper inside like a piece of rotten fruit. Her body shivered involuntarily in disgust just as the creature, no doubt in pain, pulled back and let go of her.

Sara breached the surface just before her lungs exploded, and she gulped at the air. It scorched her throat, and her chest ached with fatigue. She couldn't take any time to rest though. Kicking frantically and exaggeratedly so that nothing could catch hold again, she made it to the shore.

She stumbled to the house, bent over in both pain and terror. Her legs were weak and sticky with blood. Home was a waiting mother, heat wrapping her up like a fluffy towel. She held her arms crisscrossed in front of her trembling body. Wet hair stuck across her right eye and tickled her nose, but she dared not let go of herself to move it. If she did, surely she would fall into pieces right there on the kitchen floor.

Her purse beckoned from the table. Inside, there was a little orange bottle with a white top. On the bottle was a label with her name and her doctor's name typed on it. In the upper right corner of the label, the address to a pharmacy back in Ann Arbor. Most importantly, however, were the contents within the bottle, which were printed right smack dab in the center. *Xanax 0.5mg 1 tab by mouth, three times a day, as needed.*

Sara knew a secret: she could take more than one, more than two, even, and be okay. She further knew that she could wash those pills down with a swig or two of whiskey and, whether she wanted to or not, still wake up in the morning.

A fifth of whiskey—well, a half a fifth of whiskey—remained in the cupboard. She'd unpacked it and put it up on the top shelf, saved it for a rainy day. *Well, this is more than a rainy day, isn't it? This is a goddamned tsunami kind of day.*

She shuffled over to the cupboard, still hunched and holding her guts inside. When she felt strong enough to let go of herself, she reached for the door.

"Ick!" she cried. Dangling from the nail of her right middle finger was a long, noodley strip of flesh. Her breath stuttered out of her spasming throat. It was grotesque. She didn't want to move because, if she did, it would wriggle again like a tapeworm attached to the tip of her finger. In the slowest motion she could muster, she side-stepped, hand still held mid-air—*don't think about how you had it up against your belly just a second ago. Don't think about it or you'll lose your mind entirely, and right now, for a few more minutes, you have to keep it together*

Sara—and reached for a napkin with her free left hand. Plucking the tissue from her finger, she noted goo beneath every nail of her right hand. But the noodley tapeworm was gone. Folded inside the napkin and tossed into the garbage.

She couldn't put the Xanax off any longer. She had to calm her system, had to reabsorb some of the adrenaline souring her blood. Once the shakes subsided and her mind cleared, she would clean her nails, see to her bloodied legs, and go to bed.

"I'll think about it all tomorrow," she croaked in a terrible southern accent meant to sound like Scarlett O'Hara, then she downed three pills with as many swigs of whiskey straight from the bottle.

Chapter 24

After throwing on an old tee shirt and her nerves dulled down to a soft roar, and she felt safe sliding a wooden stick beneath her nails. She set to scraping away the monster flesh she'd acquired fighting off the attack.

In college, Sara interned at a women's shelter and carried the pager for victim's advocate. Often that meant getting called to the ER when a rape had been admitted. Her job was to go, sit with the frightened girl then walk her through the steps of the exam and evidence gathering which, for a recent victim of sexual assault, could be just as traumatizing. A part of what was commonly called the rape kit was the collection of fingernail scrapings for DNA. The process was exactly the same as what Sara currently did to herself. It was no ordinary nail cleaning; it was digging in as deep as the stick would go and scraping out every last foreign cell.

"Oh my God, DNA," she said.

She grabbed the whiskey and took a swig, congratulating herself for being able to think smartly even after her near death experience. Carrying the bottle with her, she staggered into the master bedroom where the Biology Department's equipment was stored. The Xanax was kicking in, and she felt light like a balloon. Thank goodness the whiskey put some cement in her feet. She found the box marked BIO LAB and opened it.

The contents of the box blurred in her altered state, resisting her attempts to identify the item she needed, until finally, she dumped the whole thing out onto the floor. Test tubes shattered, but that was fine. What she wanted was a small, fluid-filled plastic cup with sealable lid. She managed to snatch one after three tries—there were about a third less than her eyes told her there were—and shuffled back to the bathroom.

She tried to tweeze up all the crud she'd dropped onto another napkin. When her dexterity failed her, she folded up the whole shebang and shoved it into the cup. The paper soaked up all the preservative, but that was okay. Out in the kitchen, she had a strip of monster meat, and she was gonna send that in a separate cup. *Then they can run the test and see that I'm not crazy at all. I might even accept Andrea's apology. Wish I could see her face when Bill tells her that its mutant DNA and not some damned albino turtle.*

She should call Bill, give him a heads up. Ask for the favor which of course he would do, because first of all, he had a crush on her—always had—and secondly, he was coming there specifically to study the animal life.

It took fifteen minutes and four sips of whiskey to find her cell. Five more minutes to find Bill's number. Another five before she realized she hadn't hit the "call" button and was listening to a silent phone.

"Hello, this is Bill."

Sara giggled. Of course it was Bill. Who did he think she'd called?

"Bill, 'sme, Sara." She slurred a little and giggled again.

"Sara? Sara, are you okay? What's going on?" Worry and concern filled his voice. *He loves me. He does not love me not.*

"Jus tryinna have a swim, ya know? An I wuss attack, Bill. Sompin' pull me down and drownded me, Bill. Try to anyways. But I got free. I kicked and clawed and I got free."

"What? Sara, it's hard to understand you. Are you saying you went in the lake? Something attacked you? I'm coming there today."

"No!" she shouted and held up a hand as if he could see her. "I need you stay there. I's sen you sompin. DNA, Bill! I got DNA."

"You got a sample? What was it that attacked you?"

"Monsser, Bill. Lake Monsser. Andrea says albino snapper." She blew a raspberry. "Izz not, izz a monsser."

"Ok, Sara. Listen to me. I need you to focus. Just answer yes or no. You went swimming by yourself in the lake?"

"Yess, I tole you."

"And while you were in there, something in the lake attacked you and pulled you under?"

"Yes, Bill."

"You scratched and kicked, and you got away?"

"Yesssss." She was so tired. So tired.

"Did you get hurt?"

"My legs scratch, yeah. Be ok, Bill."

"You injured it and got some tissue? Is it dead?"

"Tissue under my nails. Iz swam away, Bill, swam away." But it had been in her house before, hadn't it? Brought the urn back and left water on her floor. She had to lock the doors and put something against the basement door. "I hafta go, Bill. I'll sen samples tomorrow."

She hung up before he could say anything else. The doors in the kitchen were so very far away, and her eyes were burning, and her legs were tired, and her lungs and throat hurt. She stumble-crawled to the couch and fell onto it. There were no more thoughts after that.

But Bill came to her anyway. He sat on the couch beside her and brushed the hair away from her face. Her eyes refused to open but, still, she knew it was him. Bill kissed her forehead and she wrapped her arms around him. He'd lost weight. His muscles were firm and youthful, skin taut and firm.

"Bill?" she whispered.

"Shh," he said and pulled her up. "Let's get these wet clothes off of you."

Hadn't she put on a dry tee-shirt? She couldn't remember. She let him sit her up and like a child, lifted her arms above her head as he slipped the shirt off.

His kisses warmed her. Hot breath rolled over her chest and abdomen like a summer fog. She ran her fingers through his thick lush hair. Not Bill. Bill's hair was thinning. And Bill had a beard—she felt none of the rough, scratchy tickle of facial hair against her breasts.

She managed to open her left eye enough to see the sandy brown mane of the man whose body pressed against hers.

"Phil?" *Is it him for real this time? Come back from the dead as his younger self?* The one that had loved her properly so many years ago? Not Phil, either. He'd never been that lean, that tan.

His hand found her middle, hot and wet, and suddenly he was inside her. She arched her back to better invite him in, still not sure of who he was. He nuzzled his face against her ear.

"It doesn't matter who I am. It is you who are. The chosen one," he said. His voice crawled into her head. "Restorer of life, savior of the harvest, daughter of Demeter."

Words thrust into her brain as he thrust his seed into her womb.

She sat up, wide awake. "Esmond?"

Early afternoon sun hit her face, and she squinted. The house was silent. Her phone beside the couch said it was 1:27 pm which meant she'd slept through the night and half a day. Her tee-shirt lay crumpled on the floor. She was naked, and her legs had bled during the blackout; they stuck to the couch in several places.

Sara let the disorientation of prolonged, drugged sleep pass. She vaguely remembered having another dream about Phil or Bill...*or Esmond?* No matter. It wasn't a nightmare about a lake monster or mole-person, so that was fine.

What was not fine was the lateness of the day and her need to get to the post office to mail the tissue from the lake monster that tried to kill her. Bill would be thrilled to have something to focus his research on. *Bill.* She had called him last night, hadn't she? The phone died as soon as she hit the recent calls app. Well, she'd call him later, after it was in the mail. But first, she needed a drink to wash what tasted like dirty cat litter out of her mouth and a shower. Her legs were tight and stiff beneath the dried blood and swollen wounds. The stairs to the shower would not be kind.

With a brown sugar cinnamon toaster pastry in her belly, coffee in a to-go mug, and her package of tissue samples, Sara fumbled the car door open and smacked her shin with the corner of the door.

"Fuck!"

She sat her precious samples floating in the necessary preservative on the front seat before seeing to the reopened gash on her leg. Blood ran hot, staining all the fresh gauze she'd just placed.

"Damnit. Ugh, I don't have time for this." Leaving the car door open, she jogged-limped back to the house.

In the middle of cleaning the wound and refreshing the gauze, it occurred to her that she did not collect any of her own blood or tissue for comparison. The last thing she needed was Andrea calling her all glib to say the tissue came from a human female with all the innuendo flowing between her words like molasses.

"Good timing, car door," she said and collected some of her blood in a phlebotomy test tube. "There, now. Let's see you all explain this away as products of my grief and solitude."

Her coffee patiently waited on the roof of the car—another reason the injury was a blessing in disguise. She'd have driven away without realizing she'd left it there. Her mind ran with so many opened tabs, she'd need to stop at some point soon and make a to-do list, trap all her thoughts and ideas on paper before they escaped into the dumpster fire of her mind.

The post office was in Vicker Valley. To avoid all the rules and questions about biohazards, she made a pit stop at Al's Drills and Pills and purchased bubble wrap, and a small glass packing kit. Once each container was wrapped securely and packed in its own little cubical, she taped up the box and shipped it off to Bill.

A young girl worked the register at Al's. Sara hadn't seen anyone else working in the store, which meant someone might be home at the Pierce's. She really wanted that picture back. It was worth a shot, at least.

Walt Pierce opened the door and looked Sara up and down, spending more than a few seconds on her bandaged legs and hands.

"So, what's the other guy look like?" he asked.

"I'm sorry?" Sara said confused.

"Looks like you got yourself in quite the fisticuffs. I'm wondering if you won or lost."

"Oh." She held her hands up. "This is all just due to a little skin condition I have. Gets pretty itchy and it's better to wrap it. The legs," she paused, unsure what to tell him and then decided to tell some of the truth. "I tried to take a swim in the lake and something attacked me. Probably a snapping turtle or something."

"You ought to be home resting. Hope you got some antibiotics. Those snappers carry all sorts of diseases."

"I have an appointment later today," she lied. "Mr. Pierce, the reason I stopped by was to see if Stephanie had a chance to show you or your wife the photograph I gave her. As you know, I'm writing a book, and some questions have come up that I think the picture might help answer."

"Still at it, eh? Well, you'd better come on in and have a seat. I'll go see if she left anything on the table for us."

The house was a typical small-town house. Two story, pale yellow, hardwood floors covered in numerous braided rag rugs. It was also a typical "grandparents' house," with crocheted lace doilies on the small round end tables, two overstuffed chairs—both sporting folded afghans on the backs—and a loveseat with large blue roses on its fabric. Silence filled the space, except for the ticking of a large grandfather clock.

"Go ahead and make yourself comfortable." Walt waved vaguely at the living room as he stomped down the hall.

Sara took in the room with its generic Home Interiors wall décor and silk flowers in vases. The brick fireplace behind the two chairs was mercifully not lit as the house was already stifling in the early August afternoon. Either they didn't have air conditioning or they chose not to utilize it—also a common grandparent's house trait. Why Stephanie still lived there made little sense. She was a real estate agent, after all. Surely she could find herself something else.

The only thing unique and personal in the entire room was the fireplace mantle covered in framed photos, awards, medals, and patches. Most were Stephanie's real estate awards. One was a fishing trophy for Walt and a blue ribbon for a quilt Bethany Pierce had won in the Wisconsin State Fair. All but one of the photos were of Stephanie at various ages. The other was a picture of Walt and Bethany at their fiftieth wedding anniversary. Sara walked along the mantle slowly, taking in each picture. The last one took her by surprise. Her heart came to a full stop just as she sucked in a gasp of air. Her body froze in time while only her eyes still moved, taking in the familiar picture of a little boy and a little girl with their arms around each other cheesing for the camera. The girl was topless and wore only baggy short pants fashioned out of a piece of bed sheet or something similar. Sara had the same picture, or one almost identical to it, at home. Julie gave it to her. The boy was Roger and the girl, Julie said, was from the commune. *Why would the Pierces have this photo on their mantle?*

128

"Don't see any pictures anywhere," Walt said. His arrival jumpstarted Sara's vital functions again, although her heart pounded hard to make up for the missed beats. "You okay?"

Sara gave her shakes a moment to settle down and ensured her legs would agree to continue to hold her weight to allow her to turn. "Yes, I just, well, this picture startled me a little."

Walt walked over to stand beside her. He took the picture down.

"Used to be, when she was little, the only chance we got to see her was at the market. This was the last picture we took of her when she still lived on the commune." He pointed to the little boy. "This is Roger McKinnon. Runs the paper. Had the biggest crush on her for the longest time. You couldn't get Stephanie alone when she came to the market, 'cause those two were joined at the hip, they were."

"I had no idea Stephanie was in the commune," Sara muttered trying to tame all the thoughts running wild in her head.

"Not something she remembers much about, and that's probably for the best." He sat the picture back on the mantle. "Stephanie usually drops in around three-thirty or four. You're welcome to wait. I can make you some tea."

"The picture I lent her, she said she intended to show it to you and see if you recognized anyone in it. It was a group of children on the commune. She seemed to think you could identify them."

"Don't know what would make her say that. Beth and I were barely allowed to see Stephanie. No one was allowed to visit the commune. Stephanie's mother, Katie, was our only child. Stephanie was three when her mother shacked up with that bunch on the hill, then everything changed. We never saw them or spoke to them after that. For a long time, they didn't come to the market on Saturdays. When she finally did, Stephanie barely remembered us."

Sara was speechless. So many questions she wanted to ask, but none of them would settle down long enough in her brain for her tongue to get hold.

"Sit, I'll make some tea." Walt said. Sara dropped into the closest chair and pulled out her phone. Technically, it would be wrong to record someone without their permission, but she had a feeling Walt wouldn't agree to let her use their conversation for her book. She'd caught him on a day when he maybe felt a little nostalgic or even wrestled with mortality. He wanted to talk, she wanted to listen. It would simply help her not miss anything he said. She hit the record button, shut off the screen and sat it on the arm of the chair. Then, thinking about the book, she stood up and snapped a picture of the picture on the mantle.

"Here we go," Walt said. He sat the tray of tea on the coffee table.

"Oh, thank you," Sara said and meant it. The warm tea would hopefully calm her nerves. She plopped a sugar cube—*who even uses sugar cubes anymore? Adorable*—into the cup and added a splash of cream. The tea pot spilled strong, black tea into her cup. The cream barely changed the liquid's deep tannic color.

"Hope you like it strong. My grandmother taught the art of tea to me. She was a proper English woman, and she liked her tea 'strong enough that a mouse could trot across the surface.' That's how I got used to drinking it. Won't take no insult to you adding more cream."

Sara took a sip. Strong as it certainly was, she detected no bitterness from over-steeping. Her grandmother used to give her Earl Grey with honey and buttered toast when she was sick, so tea always held magical powers for Sara. Her nerves immediately relaxed and she sank back into the chair.

"Mmm, it's perfect."

"Glad you think so. No, Stephanie doesn't like to talk much about her days at the commune. She was eight when she showed up here. I suspect her mother knew something was about to happen and sent her to us. We were estranged, for sure, but Katie never doubted our love for her. We would've forgiven that girl everything." He shook his head and sipped his tea.

"Do you know what happened to them? Did Stephanie tell you anything?"

"No. Don't know. I suspect it was some kind of mass suicide. Like Jonestown. I bet you, if you do some investigating in those caves, you'll find 'em."

Sara sat up. "Nobody ever looked for them? I mean, all these missing people, and no one looked in the caves or the tunnels?" *Shit. What if the monsters are just a bunch of feral children, all grown up?*

"Oh sure, a few did. Never found much. I doubt anyone looked too hard. Then, when everything up there started to die, we told ourselves they'd poisoned the land and left in the night. And we all quit worrying about it."

"Did you? I mean, Katie was your daughter."

"Katie was dead. I knew it as soon as I opened the door and saw Stephanie standing there alone. Her momma wouldn't have given her up for anything but to save her life."

"And Stephanie never talked about it?"

"Never. We got nothing out of her. She had nightmares for a while. Used to cry out in her sleep that someone stole Persephone. Someone took her. Beth and I looked into that, and you know, they called themselves Children of Demeter. Persephone—"

"Was her daughter. She was kidnapped by Hades," Sara interrupted.

"Right." Walt shrugged. "So that was no help. Probably just some nonsense that leader of theirs was preaching."

"You know, Demeter became angry with the loss of her daughter and refused to let anything grow. Even when she got Persephone back, it was only for two thirds of the year. She still has to share with Hades, and when she does, she mourns by letting everything whither up and die."

"Yep. Winter." Walt said.

"There must be some connection with Stephanie's nightmares and the sudden disappearance of the clan and the death of all life up there."

"So, who was the clan's Persephone?" Walt asked.

"Oh my God," Sara said. "What if Stephanie was Persephone? Stephanie, Persephone" She repeated the names slowly to enunciate their rhyme.

"No, they called her Moonbeam. Nothing like Persephone. Katie changed her own name to Moonstar, so I suppose that's where that nonsense came from. When she came to us, Beth told her she would have to start school the next year, and she should use her 'school name,' hoping we could get her to start thinking like a member of normal society."

Sara's phone rang, and she jumped, spilling the last sip of tea from her cup. Walt caught the cup before it tumbled off her lap. He looked into it, studying something. Caller ID notified her it was Julie. She wanted to take the call, so there was no time to ask him what he found so fascinating about her empty cup.

"I'm sorry, I have to take this." She stood, walking toward the door. "Hello?"

"Sara? Hey, it's Julie. How are you?" Julie's voice sounded strained. Her words wavered like heat coming off the sidewalk and crackled like a fire.

"Hey. Are you okay? What's wrong?"

Julie inhaled and the air audibly bounced down a staircase to her lungs. She was crying. "Roger is just furious with me for giving you those pictures. I wasn't thinking. I gave away property of the newspaper and, you know, even in the news, there are privacy policies, I guess, and…and I guess the whole disappearance is like a cold case. Meaning it's still open, sort of, and I guess, I mean, I shouldn't have let you take the pictures. I need them back as soon as possible. I'm sorry, Sara. None of this is your fault."

"Julie, oh my goodness. I mean, of course. Where can we meet?" Sara asked. She needed to tell Julie what she'd learned from Walt then help the woman calm down. She didn't have the pictures with her, and that goddamn narcissistic misogynist of a husband could come talk to her if he had any further issues about the pictures.

"Well." Julie sniffled. "Couldn't you just drop them off here at the office?"

"How about I come pick you up, and we go get a coffee and a big old donut? Carbs and caffeine are quite the cure-all."

"Oh. Ok, sure. I think I'd like that. Soon?"

"Yep, I'm just leaving the Pierce's, I'll be there in two shakes of a lamb's tale." Sara smiled. The tea had brought her grandmother's memory out of its keepsake box in her brain, causing her to use Grandma's euphemisms.

She disconnected the call and turned to Walt. "I'm sorry, Walt. Something's come up. I have to go. I really hope you'll rethink letting me interview you for the book. You've been so helpful."

"Well, again, can't say that I gave you much to work with, but I suppose I'd have to get Stephie's permission. Like I said, she don't like talking about it. Probably best not to bring it up with her, not unless she brings it up first."

"Understood. You let me know. Stephanie has my number. I'll buy you dinner for your trouble."

Walt nodded and smiled. He opened the door for her. Sara was on the porch when she remembered another question for Walt Pierce.

"Walt, have you seen this symbol before or do you have any idea what it means?" She showed him her phone with the picture of the carving from the baluster.

Walt took it in his hands for only long enough to see it. He handed it back. "Yep. That's the symbol the clan made up for Demeter. I don't think it's got any historic significance. That crazy leader of theirs, Rolf Schmidt, probably came up with it. They used to stamp it on all of their goods, labels and such. Hold on. I think I still have a couple bottles of mead with that label."

He left Sara standing on the porch. It was late August, not cold, no wind but Sara shivered anyway. She'd seen the bottles of mead, but none of them had labels. Had Stephanie peeled them off? *No. They're forty-some years old. They probably dried up and fell off.*

While she waited, she pulled up the symbols from the mural and the monsters to show him next. The creak of wooden stairs and the thuds of heavy footfall heralded his arrival back to the porch. He proudly held the bottle out to her. A yellowed, cracked label declared the bottle was Children of Demeter Clover Honey Mead and right in the center of the label was the symbol she'd just shown Walt.

"Well, then it makes sense that it is carved into my baluster and onto the lid of the well. I'll probably start finding it all over the place, now that I know what I'm looking for." She smiled and handed the bottle back to him. "Walt, can I show you a few more? These were on the mural painted on the wall in the living room." She turned the phone to him and swiped through the three close ups of symbols deciding it was best not to show him the monsters they were painted with. He took longer, closer looks at these.

"Now, I can't say that I have seen these. But like I said, that Rolf was always trying to add ways to make his beliefs more legitimate. When we first took Stephie in, she was always doodling stuff like this in her notebooks. None of these stand out or look familiar to me."

Sara sighed. "Walt, you've been such a big help. Thank you so much. Tell Stephanie I stopped by, and I hope we can get together for some lunch soon."

"I sure will, and good luck with your book."

Chapter 25

Sara bought them both mint teas and giant butter croissants. She purposefully kept the talk light and hollow while they sipped their tisanes. As a sociology major, she'd spent time in a variety of counseling centers, so she prided herself on her ability to read body language well. Julie was tense—her muscles so taut, her shoulders nearly touched her earlobes. She held her cup of tea with both hands. Out of context, perhaps with a green screen behind her putting her in the arctic, one would simply think she was freezing. But it was August, and they sat in the bakery, with its wood-fired ovens. It was cozy. As she sipped her tea and nibbled at her croissant, Julie's shoulders came down and she let go of the cup with her right hand.

"Mint helps the nerves," Sara said. Julie nodded. "Julie, I'm very sorry that Roger got so angry with you. That's not right, I hope you know. Nothing has been published, nothing has been shared with anyone. It is really no different than me coming there and looking at them with you or him. In fact, Stephanie implied that he was more than willing to help me."

"What Roger wouldn't do for Stephanie. Well, Stephanie wasn't the one who gave you the pictures. I did. So, Roger's reaction is different. That's how it goes."

Sara suddenly felt a kinship with Julie. She remembered being in Julie's position. Irritated by her husband's treatment of other women he called friends while, as his wife, she was treated like garbage—a pain he had to endure. But Julie was not yet to the acceptance phase. No matter how awful he was to her, she wouldn't yet open her eyes and see what was right in front of her—Roger and Stephanie. When she did, Sara would be there, but it wasn't the time.

"In my vast study of sociology and human interactions, I must tell you my scientific conclusions—Men suck." Sara smiled.

Julie laughed. "Well, then I don't have to feel too guilty for thinking the same thing. Since it's been scientifically proven and all."

"Time and again, sister. Time and again." They both laughed then.

"So, listen. Julie, I don't have the pictures with me." Julie's shoulders shot right back up to her ears. "Whoa. It's okay. Just tell him you called me and left a message. He doesn't know you're meeting with me right now, does he?"

"No." She shook her head. "He's at Roy's today, helping with the corn. I told everyone else I was going for a walk."

"Good. So much has happened since we spoke. I don't even know where to begin, but I need you to just keep an open mind, and maybe don't interrupt until I get everything out."

"Okay," she said and then picked up her croissant stuffed half of it in her mouth and bit. "I ant awk ow."

Sara rolled her eyes at her friend's silliness and began.

The tea was gone and only crumbs remained when Sara finished with the Stephanie/Persephone connection.

"Okay, let me start by saying that while I agreed not to interrupt, I can't agree with this idea. Sara, that cannot be Stephanie in that picture. No way. I mean, Roger said he didn't know who it was. He said…" Her voice trailed off as she began to put pieces together. "It *can't* be her."

"I mean, comparing her picture to others they had on the mantle, it's her all right, even if we can't trust Walt Pierce. Although, I think we can."

"I don't know how to confront Roger with all this."

"Don't! Not yet. Julie, we need to get a little more info before we say anything. Besides, Roger and Stephanie have been friends for a long time, and Walt said it upsets her to talk about it. Maybe he is just keeping her secret because he knows it stirs up bad memories. Maybe that's why he got so mad. If he had been the one to 'help' me, he would have chosen which pictures I could see and which I couldn't. You know?"

Julie nodded. She wanted to believe the alternative theory, so it was easy to convince her.

"Tell Roger you called me several times and left messages, but I haven't called you back."

"How long does it take DNA results to come back?" Julie asked changing the subject. Clearly, she didn't relish lying to her husband, but she would. Sara could see it in her eyes.

"Well, first Bill will do basic cellular examinations just to try to identify what species that thing is. Then, if needed, he'll do DNA testing."

"So probably it'll take a while, then?" She was asking how long she had to keep secrets from her husband. The longer she lied and kept the truth from him, the worse her punishment would be. Sara saw those thoughts as easily as if they'd been on a news banner scrolling across Julie's forehead.

"There is nothing Bill loves more than a mystery. Believe me. To be honest, he's always had a thing for me. My friend Andrea thinks I am going crazy up here and hallucinating everything. So, Bill is caught between the both of us. He'll work day and night to get scientific, indisputable answers to settle the disagreement as fast as possible. I bet we'll have results in a week at most."

Julie nodded in thought. Her phone buzzed and Sara saw Roger's name pop up with a message: *WHERE R U?*

"Shit, Sara. I totally lost track of the time. Can you drop me off at Al's? I'll call him from there. I'll tell him I silenced my phone and went for a walk. He'll buy it. It's what I usually do when we fight."

"Absolutely. Let's get you back."

The smells coming out of Slim's when she let Julie out of the car made her mouth water for a full meal. *It is well past five, might as well go have some dinner before heading home.* She could use the alone time to write some notes.

Two cups of tea coupled with a lot to think about put her in the mood for a beer, a nice dark stout and a big plate of fattening poutine. While she waited for her food, Sara dabbled on her phone, checking social media—all the same shit and ignorant arguments against science—and her news app, which was filled with the usual uproar over the newest political buffoonery.

"Blah." She tossed her phone on the table.

It was late for the dinner rush and the place was fairly quiet, only a couple families finishing up their meals. Gail brought her poutine and offered to refill her beer.

"Oh no, I have to drive home yet."

"Gotta hand it to ya, girlfriend. You've made it a hell of a lot longer than anyone thought you would up there all alone. Stephanie says the house likes you, and I guess it must, cause everyone else says it's haunted."

"I don't think it's haunted." *More like infested.* She didn't speak the last part of the thought, though.

"You'd be the only one, and I'll take your word for it," Gail laughed. "Can I bring you some water or iced tea?"

"Water would be great, Gail. I've reached my max on tea today."

Gail left her to the steaming plate of French-fried gluttony smothered in viscous, beefy, artery-clogging heaven. Sara's stomach lurched hungrily at the smell. She picked off a couple cheese curds with her fingers and popped them in her mouth. Molten lava. She chewed with her mouth wide open, pulling air in and out to cool them before bringing her tongue back into the act.

The door swung open and a man walked in—tall, tan-skinned, mid-life belly bulge, and light brown hair speckled with gray peeked out beneath his ball cap. His matching close-cut beard couldn't hide the scowl as he surveyed the place.

"Hey there, Rog," Gail called out. "Go ahead and pick a seat anywhere. Just you tonight?

The muscles in Sara's chest spasmed, stopping the curds' journey through her esophagus toward her stomach. She tried to cough but thought better of it. Best not call any attention to herself. The door swung open just behind him, and Julie let herself in. The bastard hadn't waited or held the door for his own wife. Why did everyone in this town seem to like the guy so much?

"Me too, Gail!" Julie called. It was sad to see the educated woman brought to the level of a bully's sycophant. Sara dropped her head, hoping that Julie wouldn't see her, and worked on the plate of poutine.

Julie and Roger chose a table far enough away that Sara couldn't make out their words, but the pressured tone, Roger's leaning across the table into Julie's space, and his clenched muscles left no doubt as to the topic at hand. When Gail came over with drinks and her tablet to take their order, Roger immediately relaxed, sat back in his seat and smiled. *Classic behavior of the narcissist.*

Julie's sniffles could be heard easily through the whole establishment, although everyone pretended not to notice. She showed her phone to her husband, shrugged her shoulders, and shook her head. Sara had seen quite enough. She tossed a twenty on the table, thought better of it, and added a five before she headed over to meet the famous Roger McKinnon.

"Julie?" she said, approaching the table. Julie looked up, and her bloodshot eyes widened. *Play along with me.* Sara sent the thought telepathically. "Hey, it's so funny to see you here. I had a bunch of errands to run today and just had the chance to check my messages. I got yours, and was going to run home just now and check for those pics."

"Oh," Julie laughed. "Yes. I—"

Sara interrupted, "I bet I accidentally gathered some of the newspaper ones with my own when I got that call and had to leave so quick, remember?"

Julie's mouth hung open like a dead fish. She nodded.

"Truth is, I haven't even looked in the envelope since then. I've been so busy unpacking and painting. Goodness, I feel awful. Wouldn't want you to think I was a thief. I've been in research long enough, I should've known better than to be so casual about packing up."

"Oh, well, I mean, that call you got. You said something about an emergency. So, it's completely understandable." *She caught on. Good.* "Oh! Sara, you've never officially met Roger, have you?"

Sara put her hand out and grinned a honey-sweet toothy grin. "No, we haven't unfortunately. But Stephanie sings your praises so often, I feel like I know you." *There, a little passive-aggressive introduction never hurt anybody.*

"Great to finally meet you. Roy has a lot to say about you, too." *Touché.*

"So, yeah. I stopped by the other day hoping to find you. Stephanie said you would be super helpful and that you had a lot of pictures and news of the Demeter's Children clan. But you were out, so Julie was kind enough to take your place. You'd never know she wasn't owner and operator. You're very lucky to have someone so well educated and knowledgeable to run things when you aren't able to be there." She enjoyed their little volley more than she should.

"Unfortunately, she is not as mindful and observant as the owner and operator. Otherwise, you wouldn't need to make another trip to town just to drop off our property."

"Oh, no worries about that. You're such a busy man, I was starting to think I'd have to drive to town everyday just to find you at work. I even wondered if you were avoiding me," Sara laughed. It was a real laugh, but she tried to make it sound light and meaningless. A jolt of pleasure hit her system at the color flushes on his face every time she pitched his snark right back at him.

"No, no. It's just some of us didn't fall into a bucket of money big enough to run away and write a book. I mean, a doctor's life insurance policy must be worth at least a million, right? I have to work two jobs to keep us in the green. I figured you might take some time to mourn before rushing into your research. Most widows do, anyhow."

"Roger!" Julie reached out and gave his hand a squeeze. "That's a terrible thing to say. I'm sorry, Sara. Roger's had a bad day; he didn't mean that."

"It's fine, Julie." Sara patted Julie's shoulder before turning her attention back to Roger. "I don't take the time to mourn cheaters and liars, Mr. McKinnon, and as my late husband's insurance illustrates, you can't buy decency. I'll bring your photos by tomorrow, Julie." *There.* She had nothing more to say to the jackass.

She suppressed her giggle until she got to her car. Hopefully, Julie wouldn't bear the aftermath of Sara's little game. That was the only somber thought the rest of the way home.

Lightning bugs gave the illusion that all the stars had fallen from the sky and floated about on earth. A new moon offered nothing through the cloud cover that rolled in with the night. Sara used her phone's flashlight app to see her way through the stone arch and across the yard to the house. She'd forgotten to turn on the porch lights before she'd left. Every step stole more of her mirth and replaced it with paranoia. Was someone following her? Did she hear breathing to her left? Was that the splash of a body emerging from the lake to her right?

She picked up her pace until she jogged the last few feet to the front porch and up the five concrete steps. She fumbled her keys from her pocket and felt like some dumb girl from a horror movie. The light shook and she juggled the keyring one-handed, trying to find the right one. Yes, there was someone out on the lawn. She heard the soft crush of grass of footfalls coming closer.

She could swing the light toward the noise, perhaps temporarily blinding her stalker, and give herself a chance to see what she was up against. Instead, like a child fighting the fear of the monster under their bed, she decided not looking was the better strategy.

Finally, the key slid home and the knob turned effortlessly. Sara hurled herself inside, slammed the door, and locked it. She turned the porch light on and looked out the front window of the master bedroom/equipment storage room. Nothing out there. No movement in the trees to suggest a breeze, no shadows, and no monsters.

"Tea before beer makes monsters appear." She laughed at her cleverness with words and rhymes over the last few hours. Figuratively patting herself on the back, she climbed the stairs toward her room. There was a lot to think about, but her brain had locked up shop and put up the "closed for business" sign.

Chapter 26

The most restful sleep only brought the morning quicker, or at least Sara thought so as she awakened. She peeled the gauze off her legs and left hand. Her wounds were healing quickly, but the new skin was so pink and fragile, almost purple against her pasty-white Michigan tone.

Hot water poured over her in the shower, reviving her mind and body. Even her scrapes and scratches accepted the sensation without stinging protest. Sara stepped out feeling lighter than she had in days. Answers were coming. For the first time since she'd moved in, she felt that she finally had all the pieces to the puzzle in one box. All she had to do was put them together.

Oatmeal with blueberries and orange juice wouldn't make up for a day filled with fattening carbs, but it was a start. She spread out the pictures on the table and studied each one with intensity as she ate her breakfast. She and Julie had put a sticky note on the back of each picture with a corresponding number. On the notebook paper, beside each number, was a list of names. They'd managed to identify the majority of people in the pictures. Sara found Merry Dai easily enough. Those eyes more so than anyone else's always seemed look right into Sara's soul—a sense of déjà vu every time she saw the woman's picture or name. She remembered Julie saying Merry looked like a teenage version of herself. That, she couldn't see…maybe the eyes, though.

Moving on. Another picture depicted a new mother, who they'd identified as Harvest Eve. She held a single baby in her arms, but no joy on her face. Her eyes, unlike Merry's, never focused on the camera; instead, she appeared to be considering something only she could see. Something far off on the horizon, perhaps. *Postpartum depression, most likely.*

Sara grabbed the ledger and pulled it over. Flipping toward the front, she found Harvest's name listed under the heading *Cross-Over*. On November 5,1969, Harvest had a number two written in her row, yet only one baby in her arms, and she didn't seem happy about it. Sara scanned page after page, searching for a single birth for the young mother, but the girl's name didn't appear again.

"So much for the twin theory." Sara said took her bowl to the sink.

Movement outside the window by the table caught her attention as she sat back down to study. The field that just yesterday was a muddy, swampy dead-patch was gone. In its place, an acre of wild grasses and poppies waved in the breeze—red poppies, everywhere. Rabbits hopped about nibbling the green and red vegetation, their ears perked on alert at all times. Not a one was dirty with mud, none seemed to have any evidence of feet stuck in the muck.

If she wanted it, Sara had a straight, unhindered path to the caves on the other side. To the caves where Walt was certain she would find the remains of a mass suicide.

"I guess old Roger can wait a little longer for these pictures," she said.

Rain drizzled on her as she headed toward the caves. She was halfway across the field before she thought that she should have put on long pants if she intended to climb around inside the earth. She didn't want to chance an infection, but after a momentary pause, Sara decided things changed around the property far too fast to trust that it would still be solid ground when she returned. Best just to keep going, chance an infection, and wash up well as soon as she got back.

There were three caves to choose from, but Sara didn't need any time for contemplation. Roy's story and the wall mural pointed to the third and largest as the altar bearer. She went inside. The mildewed smell of damp rags lingered beneath the scent of recently burnt candles. Indeed, on the altar which stood directly opposite the entrance of the cave, two half-burned candles sat, one on each end. Rolled up woven mats lined the walls just as Roy had described. They looked as if they hadn't been touched or moved in forty some years. Sara bet, if she'd tried to unroll one, it would disintegrate. They didn't matter, though. What mattered was the small rectangular one at the base of the altar. Even more important were the offerings sitting between the candles on the altar.

The rag rug with its strips sewn together and fringed out on each end, much like the one her grandmother kept in front of the kitchen sink, was not forty-some years old. Maybe twenty? Dirty and faded, but in one piece, the rug had two linear indentations in its middle which corresponded with knees pressed upon it in supplication. Kneeling on the rug, everything was at eye level. Fresh ears of corn, dried wheat bundles, bottles of mead, grapes, blackberries, blueberries, a pomegranate and apples. Sara picked up an apple—fresh. Behind it, a white cord snaked around the harvest. Fishing it out, she discovered her headphones.

"What the fuck?" She sat the apple down. It fell off the altar and rolled into the divot made by her knees. A sticker declaring it a Red Delicious variety gave it away as a store-bought "harvest."

"Someone's playing games." She stood up and began moving all the items to search for anymore pilfered belongings. Threaded onto the husk of a peeled cob of corn, she found her wedding band—the one she'd thrown in the lake on her first day at Demeter House.

"No!" she screamed then threw the bunch of corn and swiped the rest of the altar clean.

"Aack," The noise bounced off the walls of the cave.

Sara jumped. There were two openings—one on either side of the altar—presumably tunneling back into the cave system. The entrance to her left appeared empty but, in the right one, three sets of eyes glowed. One set inched closer, stepping over the ruined offering at its feet. Sara watched, frozen in place as the small creature approached on all fours. *Feral children.* The creature looked like a bald Mowgli from *The Jungle Book*, with elongated bat-like ears, and a gray-blue skin tone. Round, milky eyes bulged from lidless orbits. The two others behind it inched closer, too.

"My god," Sara whispered.

The leader opened his—*her? its? No genitalia at all*—mouth showing off tiny needle teeth that filled the space around a small tubular tongue like a hummingbird's.

"Aack," it said again, and Sara ran.

Chapter 27

The tunnel quickly coned downward, so by the time the first branch appeared, Sara was on her hands and knees. She held her phone up in her left hand for light. Instinct told her to take the new path, but she overrode it and kept going until another showed up. She took that one, which veered to the left and then curved to the left again. She tried to keep a map in her head and thought she faced the house again, but she couldn't be sure. The walls of the tunnel were slick and wet and it sloped deeper into the earth.

Closer to Demeter. No, that's crazy. There is no Demeter, and there are no monsters. This whole thing is some elaborate prank, probably orchestrated by the town to run off anyone who asks too many questions. Roger, who supposedly is always helping Roy, could be doing it while Roy distracts me. Or Stephanie? Maybe she doesn't want anyone to find out about her own past. Hell, for all I know, even Julie and Gail could be playing a part.

The diameter of the tunnel narrowed and forced her on her belly to army crawl, but it wasn't so tight that she felt trapped. She was trapped, though. There was no way to turn around. The only option was to keep going forward. Her own ragged breathing was all she could hear, but she didn't dare stop to listen for the feral cave children.

So, who's playing the role of monster children, Sara, huh? If this is all a ruse, then who could fit into a bodysuit like that? Hard enough to find one, let alone three kids to agree to that.

Okay, then, which of the monsters are strolling into the grocery store to buy apples for the altar? The Mole Man? The Lake Thing? Maybe the little cave beasts pile up in a trench coat and pretend to be a grown up?

You're losing it. Now is not the time to lose it, Sara. Don't even try to make sense of it until we're out of here.

She felt the bandage on her left leg slide off, but there was nothing to be done about that. *Just keep going.* If she was guessing distance right—and who knew based on belly crawls—she was only halfway across the field. She would not take a side branch until she was closer to where she thought the house might be. She hadn't noticed that the light on her phone had dimmed until it was gone completely and she was pitched into pure darkness. The rest of her senses went into overdrive, and the scent of fishing worms consumed the coffin-sized space. Everything at that point was done by touch.

Now who's the Mole Man?

Oh my god, shut up.

The width of the tunnel remained consistent, at least, which gave her hope. It was cool and, yes, there was an occasional piece of root that left a scratch, but the walls for the most part were smooth. *That's because they've been used for the last forty years. Are you ready to meet the next mutant creature? The human earthworm? Of course, you can't see a thing, so you won't see him coming. You'll just feel his slimy, featureless face when you bump your own into it.*

You're not helping. Seriously. Why do you have to be such a traitor?

Before she could respond to herself, the tunnel turned ever so slightly, and vision improved. There was some light ahead. Her arms burned in protest, but she increased her pace. The tunnel widened, and Sara found she could get up on her hands and knees again. Her stiff joints screamed in protest.

As the space enlarged, the floor got rougher. Beneath her palms, Sara could tell straw had been strewn about. Some of the drier pieces stabbed at her legs and, when she entered a small cavern of sorts, her right leg's bandage fell off.

Sara paid it no mind because she had entered a nest. Here, the ground was covered with straw and indentations—a nest. The light came from the open slab of the well cover. Rain, which had been falling so slightly when she went into the cave—*a million years ago*—poured down the thirty foot cylinder like a shower for giants. Sara rubbed her bare arms and allowed her eyes to fully adjust to the light.

This space was the Grand Central Station of subterranean travel at Demeter house. Six tunnels branched off in no particular symmetry. The one Sara had traversed clearly led back to the caves, and the one beside it ran in the same direction—likely it ended there, too. She guessed one would take its inhabitant to the lake, the next to the root cellar, one out to the greenhouses, or perhaps as far as the road itself. The other appeared to veer off toward Kumpula farm. *Maybe that's how Roy's been spying on me all this time?*

"Sure, the old man is what? Sixty-five, almost seventy? He's probably belly-crawling through here all the time, reliving his glory days of the war." She rolled her eyes at her thoughts. As she did, something—just a flash—caught her eye. Between the lake tunnel and the house tunnel, a small vase leaned against the wall, its cap, trimmed in gold peeked above the straw that had been strategically placed to cover it. *Phil's urn.*

Sara spun around and eyed the floor of the well, soaked by the rainfall and giving off the cloying stink of decay. No way had the thing hit bottom and rolled the entire way across the burrow before making a last-minute turn to rest against the dirt wall. Someone or some*thing* had moved it. She brushed away the straw which uncovered an almost empty bag of granola and a lidless jar of peanut butter that appeared to have been eaten using only long, grubby fingers.

"These are my snacks!" Sara heard the whine in her voice. As if this was a sibling's room, and she'd just found they'd hidden her things there, instead of in an underground network of human-sized tunnels.

Phil's urn leaned solemnly against the wall, having come to the understanding that she was not there to rescue it. The thing had taken on Phil's personality in Sara's stressed mind. She saw him bouncing his head against the wall ever so slightly the way he did when he was thinking or bored or feeling alone. She'd always found it cute in a child-like way, his only display of human emotional weakness. His little harmless head bounces.

The urn didn't bounce and, to Sara, it was all just fake, anyway. Phil faking normal human repentance, normal human shame. She knew better. She wasn't going to fall for it this time.

"I don't want you back anymore. Sit there and look pathetic all you like."

The grumble-moan she'd initially assigned to the Phil-urn as a response to her admonishment actually came from the tunnel to its right—the one that she'd guessed led to the house. The one she was steeling herself to take in the dark to get home.

Sara held her breath. Grunts, sighs, and wheezes echoed into the chamber where she stood wide-eyed and terrified. She backed up several steps until the rain began to send its spittle out to tickle her. Things waited in the tunnels. Things, as in more than one. Without nearing the openings, she couldn't tell exactly which branch her pursuers would spill from and she had no intention of meeting one face-to-face on their turf.

Sara walked into the waterfall of the well. Her foot landed on what she assumed was a round stone, but when she put her weight into the step, it cracked, and her foot crashed onto the uneven ground beneath it. Ligaments screamed in protest as her ankle rolled unnaturally away from the ends of her leg bones, which kept moving with forward momentum.

She cried out in pain and surprise. The sound did nothing to deter whatever creatures came for her. In fact, their frenzied grunts and squeaks increased in volume and intensity.

"Shit," she whispered. She worked her aching joint in small circles to pop it back to factory settings.

If she spread her legs out, one on each wall, and spider-walked up thirty feet to the top, she'd be home free. Time, rain, and darkness had made every vertical surface slimy and slick. Her fingers dug into the wet muck of the sides and found purchase in the space between ancient cobblestones and lake rocks that had once formed the sides of a working well.

Don't look back, just focus on the light. That worked for less than ten seconds before big plump drops of water glazed her eyes. It was like some twisted form of water torture. She tilted her head and tried to wipe her face dry with the shoulder of her tee-shirt, but it did nothing to improve her murky vision.

The scratching and grunting sounds bounced around the empty space until Sara couldn't distinguish which direction they came from, only that multiple creatures were getting close—much too close for someone who was only about three feet off the ground. Her heart pounded and each pull of blood into its chambers seemed to draw all her air in as well, like a bellows. *Climb, climb, climb.*

She watched her fingers find purchase on stone edges and convinced herself that, if she kept her focus on the stone, nothing could slip. Each hand was a parent, choosing the path carefully, considering each inch. Her feet skipped one after the other, quick and small, like toddlers following behind, hopping in puddles and hoping to stay upright.

When the mole creatures reached the base of the well, Sara had gained three more feet of height. Their wheezy excitement buzzed below her, but if she even dared to hazard a look, she'd fall. A rough hand swept at her ankle just as she'd let go of her right hand to reach for the next stone. Instinct and fear worked instantaneously, and she kicked out at the harasser.

Sara's mind had a split second to understand that she was falling before her head hit the ground hard. Until that moment, she'd always thought the seeing stars and hearing birds after a hard bump on the head was just cartoon fodder, but she couldn't see a thing until the fireworks settled into dying embers. As the shock of the fall dissipated, her body took inventory of her injuries. Left knee: dislocated cap and possible torn ligaments, right ring finger: sprained or maybe broken, head: concussed, possibly fractured. Baby pig noises to her left helped her orient herself. She turned to face them—what else could she do? She wasn't going anywhere.

The face that stared back at her from mere inches away didn't look like a mole or a fish or some demonic cave creature. It was a tiny pus-colored ghost with a toothless scream of terror frozen for eternity. Sunken, hollow eyes in a skull the size of a large grapefruit tried to warn her. Beyond the tiny cranium, a group of five, maybe six adult-sized beings whispered in an insectile nonsense chant. Teeth, long and thin, almost glowed in the fading light of a summer afternoon rainstorm.

"You should try to get away," the newborn's skull warned her. Sara wasn't sure if the thing had actually spoken to her or if her battered brain was using the remains to speak to a body that no longer responded to commands.

"I can't, can't hardly move," she told the long-dead child.

"But there are already too many babies here," the little head sobbed.

The creatures approached. Sara watched them in slow motion. They would tear her apart, maybe just start eating her right then and there. Would it hurt, to be eaten alive? How long could she last before death released her? She hoped they'd tear into her neck before her guts. If she had to watch them disembowel her and then begin eating, she'd go mad.

148

Her right hand rested on a stone—maybe she'd pulled it out during her fall. Maybe it was what broke her finger when she'd landed. That finger throbbed as if in response to the sudden attention it was getting. She wrapped her four remaining digits around it and found it was much lighter than she expected. Perhaps it would still work to scare the monsters off.

She never had a chance. The "rock" rolled down her arm and landed on her chest before she could launch it at the creatures. A twin to the skull beside her looked at her from her chest, only its jaw was gone so, unlike its sibling, this one could do nothing to warn Sara away from the wheezing, snorting things coming to eat her all up.

Hands, claws, appendages of unknown varieties descended upon her. Pulling at her clothes, jiggling her useless body, dragging her further into their den and away from her only chance of escape.

Any second, she'd feel those long syringe-like incisors pierce her skin. A dirt-caked claw would drag across her stomach, spilling her vitals for all to share. The dam broke and adrenaline flooded her muscles. The ability to move returned, and she fought against the clutches of the subterranean carnivores. She drew in a breath and opened her mouth to scream.

The screech that tore through space and scraped at eardrums like nails on a chalkboard did not come from within Sara. The crowd of flesh mongers retreated to the far walls of the cavern. Pushing through the crowd came a larger, fleshier version of the mole people. They hissed and grunted at her but she ignored them. Sara rolled herself up into a sitting position and scooted herself backwards with her good leg. The creature approached, hunched over like a rodent Quasimodo, the tips of her claws brushing the ground.

"No. No. You get away from me," Sara rasped.

The thing paid no mind. Sara's back hit the stony wall of the well, and she used it to push herself up onto her right leg. The creature screeched again but in a lower, longer pitch. Sara chanced a limp on her left leg in order to take a swing at the mutant. Bones beneath her already unsteady feet shifted and she fell. Her attacker reached out for her, but Sara batted her away.

This time, her head made contact with the floor just above and behind her left ear. Her vision tunneled and the light at the top of the well decreased to a hole the size of a pinhead. Just before the darkness engulfed her entirely, a warm, soft hand caressed her cheek. The monster's face looked back at her as if through the wrong side of a telescope. Even at the strange close-up distance, Sara saw no malice or hunger in the creature's eyes. What she saw, instead, was a reflection of her own.

And, then, nothing at all.

Chapter 28

Needles bored into Sara's fingers while some invisible force held her in a Vulcan death grip. Consciousness was not kind. The pain kept her eyes shut tight while proprioception returned to her body. She lay flat, not on a bed or on a cushion, but also not on the ground. Both arms stretched over her head and, based on her grumbling nerves, had been so for some time. Her head ached and either rested on a large lump of whatever bedding lay beneath her or she had quite the goose egg. Judging by the tenderness and the memory of hitting it hard when she fell, the lump would be coming with her when she sat up. She made a fist; her right ring finger was swollen and it screamed in protest but it did concede, leading Sara to believe that it was not broken. She needed to get up, to test the knee, do a full body assessment of injuries sustained.

Sitting up, though, was not going to happen right away. None of her muscles were willing to work with her just yet; instead, they insisted on crying out their grievances about being left in the same position for who knew how long. Fresh but warm air kissed her face, and she realized she was no longer in a dirt tunnel.

The face, the eyes of the mole-person, flashed through her mind. The others, the one's who'd grabbed at her and pulled her back down, were animals, feral and inhuman. But the one—the dissenter—her eyes were so familiar, so kind.

Sara hazarded a peek. There was light, but it was dim and unaggressive. She was in the old greenhouse, in the corner on the pile of hay. Slowly and with determination, she brought both arms down to her sides. Her shoulders were rusty hinges frozen in place for centuries. Ratcheting back into a more anatomic position, her nerves set fire to her arms. Stretching her neck to relieve the muscle-ache, she turned her head. Beside her and outlining her body like a murder scene, was a ring of mushrooms that must have sprouted in the time she'd been lying there.

How long have I been here?

Her stomach grumbled in reply. The hollow in her belly and a cotton-dry mouth suggested perhaps she had been there for centuries. The mushrooms with their long, thin stalks and plump, brown heads looked familiar. *Shitakes, maybe?* Were they safe to eat? She rolled to her side. A tinkling sound accompanied her movement and the cool metal that brushed over her breast caught her attention. Dog tags. She wore dog tags. In the gloom of the greenhouse and with her blurred, post-concussion vision, she couldn't read them. Besides, the idea of mushrooms sautéed in butter and garlic seemed more important than how she got there or where the dog tags came from.

Let's put off thinking about the colony of mole-people living beneath the house or about the tiny skulls at the bottom of the well until after I'm strong enough to cope with it.

Sara sat up and waited for the world to stop spinning before she plucked a mushroom. She sniffed it, licked it, and took a tiny Alice-sized nibble in case it made her shoot up so large that she broke through the glass of the house. The taste was divine. No hint of bitterness that might make her hesitate. She popped the whole thing in her mouth and savored the chewy, earthy flavor. They certainly didn't have the umami flavor of shitakes or morels, but they weren't sour or bitter like she'd expect poisonous mushrooms to taste. Her stomach lurched for more. Initially, her intent had been to take some to the house and cook them, but suddenly, she was ravenous. She picked them hand to mouth until half her outline was gone and she felt well enough to get up. Her knee took the weight without much protest. If it had been dislocated, it must have popped back in place during her journey to the greenhouse. Sore, certainly, but strong enough to walk home, she got up and focused on a mental list of tasks ahead. She'd get a drink, clean herself up, assess her wounds, and then come back out for the rest of the mushrooms.

The front door sported a bright yellow square that, upon closer inspection, was a sticky note left by Stephanie.

Stopped by to drop off that picture. Saw your car, but no answer. Waited here for about half an hour. Hope you're okay. Call me when you can.

Stephanie.

Sara pulled the note down and carried it in the house. She would deal with that later, too. The walk from the greenhouse had used up all the energy she'd gotten from the mushrooms and she was famished. Crackers and granola by the handful followed by two full glasses of tap water and a cold cola started to fill her belly. She was working the can opener on some tuna when she noticed her dirt-caked nails.

On further inspection, she was entirely crusted with dried mud. Perhaps the tuna salad sandwich could wait until after a shower. There was no need to track anymore mud through the house, either. She stripped out of everything, throwing the dog tags on the table, and headed through the living room toward the stairs. How long had it been since she'd walked around barefoot in the house? The floor was noticeably uneven. It undulated like waves beneath her. In fact, the walls undulated, too.

The exuberant swirls of the mural accentuated the illusion of movement. Sara stared, transfixed by the way the colors changed as if by seasons—trees rolling from green to orange to brown to bare and back to green again. Spots of red mottled the green until they fell away and turned brown themselves.

The ring of dancers around the well fell into a frenzy of movement. Dancer's bellies grew plump until the plumpest stepped out of the ring, nearer to the well, and squatted. Two babies, one after another, slid from her womb in a splash of red. One child raised her hand, which revealed a stamp much like Sara's birthmark. The mother scooped the unmarked baby into her arms. A man—tall, with curly blonde hair—broke through the ring of dancers and lifted the unwanted child. Sara had seen him before—he'd come to her once in a dream, then made love to her. What was he doing with the baby? She watched, terrified, as he held the child above his head before tossing her into the well. The dancers stopped and fell to their knees as both he and the baby's mother did as well.

Chanting erupted from the wall. "Praise be to Demeter, to her daughters, to her children. May she bless us with her maternal grace."

They all turned to Sara, as if they could see her just as easily as she could see them. "Come, Sara, daughter of Demeter. Come, dance with us. Come, give yourself to the Goddess. Fulfill your destiny and bring life once more to this barren land."

The curly haired man beckoned. "Come, Sara. Come."

The group of women repeated, "Come, Sara. Come."

Their request filled her ears like the roar of the ocean. She would. She would come and be a child of Demeter. She rode the waves of the living house, and it washed her out to the kitchen door. Naked and unafraid, she practically floated to the well. She couldn't see them anymore, the dancers, but she could hear them as they chanted praise to the Goddess and to Sara herself, their savior. She who would bring life back to the commune, she who would bring all the children of Demeter home.

"Come Sara. Come," the children called to her from the bottom of the well.

"Come Sara. Come," the babies, marked by the Goddess, called.

Her toes rested at the edge of the opening, curling over the edge.

"Sara! Wait!" a voice called. She wavered, wanting nothing more than to join the oblivion at the bottom of the well.

The moonlight outlined a figure as it approached her. She held her hands out to him, teetering on the edge of the well, babies calling out to her, their sister, Demeter's daughter, to come, come, come.

He reached her just as her muscles gave, and she began to fall forward. His strong arms caught her up, and he held her like a groom who carried his bride over the threshold. She gave herself to him. Letting him lift her body as he had the baby chosen by the Goddess, she resigned herself to her fate and, in doing so, smiled knowing she would bring life back to the children, the land, and Demeter Herself.

Chapter 29

The gorge rose up without warning. It wasn't until the spasm brought the vomit out and all over her, that Sara came to.

"Uh oh! Well, better out than in my ma always said," the voice, decidedly male and familiar, said.

Sara's head sent drum signals warning her not to open her eyes, but she cracked them enough to see the curls outlined by the sun. *Esmond.*

Her own voice was weak and raspy. "Why did you stop me? Isn't that what you wanted?"

"Why would I want you dead, when everything I've done was to keep you alive?" he asked.

Why? She couldn't think. Hadn't he told her she was meant to be there? Hadn't he called her to be with him and fulfill her destiny?

"But I'm marked like the babies. I'm supposed to die." She held her hand up. The bandage long gone somewhere underground, the scab crusted with dirt, fresh vomit, and snot. He pulled his shirt off and wiped her clean, gently pushing her hand back down by her side.

"Maybe so, but you're not meant to die here. Not under my watch." He worked an arm under her head.

"I don't know what to do next. What am I supposed to do? You said I was the chosen one."

Before he could answer, she vomited again. All over him, as he squatted beside her. Instead of pushing away in disgust, he swept her up into his arms.

"Right now, let's focus on getting you healthy both physically and mentally, then I guess you'll figure it out. You're a smart lady, like your mother. I know you'll find the answers on your own." He stopped talking to breathe heavy as he carried her up the stairs toward the bathroom.

Once inside, he stood her up with her arms around his neck for support and filled the tub.

"Let's get you cleaned up."

Sara sunk into the warmth of the water and let Esmond wash away her worries.

Cool water kissed her lips and she opened them. She accepted the drink, only then realizing how dry she felt. She guzzled, grabbing at the glass with both hands as a baby might. But her nurse held tight to the glass.

"Whoa, there, don't want to bring it all back up again." He said as he pulled it away and then wiped the dribble off her chin.

Where was she? Someplace warm and comfortable. She peeked but it was dark. A thin silhouette of a man sat on her bedside; his face hidden in the shadows of night. He reached out and brushed her hair from her eyes before tucking it behind her ear. *Phil.*

"Why'd you leave me?" she whispered.

"I didn't want to, but I had no choice, or at least I didn't think I did." He gave her another sip of water. She took it.

"But why her? Couldn't you have told me? You should have told me from the start." Her voice cracked. Her throat was so dry, and crying would only make it swollen and sore. She tried to swallow the hurt away.

"I know. I know. I thought I loved her. I thought I was doing the right thing by you and by her. And I thought it was better to try to drive you away instead of trying to explain myself. Didn't think you'd believe me."

The tears came, the lump in her throat threatened to close off her breathing, and her stomach offered to send the water she'd just drunk back up. "You stole everything from me. My life, my job, my identity. How can I mourn your loss when I hate you so much? You even took that away. I hate you."

He nodded, hearing her pain and maybe internalizing it. She wanted him to carry it with him to his grave. Take her pain and drag it into whatever afterlife he might have.

156

"Shhh. It's okay. You have every right to hate me, but right now, I want you to rest. You need to rest, okay? When you're feeling better, I promise to tell you everything. It's time to tell you everything."

She felt the cool glass on her lips again. She took a drink, and then let herself fall back into oblivion.

Chapter 30

She is back in the lake, swimming. The water is warm and inviting and calm, so very calm. The lake is big, and she is naked and tiny but unafraid. She falls beneath the surface, and she finds that she needs no air. She can lie within the abyss, deprived of all senses. Except there is something. The waves, perhaps, or a current beneath the surface thumping in a rhythm that is soothing. She sinks lower and lower.

Something scratches at her heel, and then again at her other foot. More scrapes at her ankles—like cold sticks brushing against her. But no, not sticks, because sticks don't bend on their own. They touch her and curl against her. So many now both feet are enveloped in firm, cold, bony fingers. They wrap around her toes and her heels and the sides of her feet. One is pinching at her Achilles tendon, and they all pull. She is dragged to the bottom, pulled deeper and deeper, and then she is falling. She has burst through the bottom of the lake and now she is falling through the air. Red clouds flash past her, and she lands hard on the rocky earth. But the rocks are moving, crawling out from under her. She looks around for escape, but someone has tilted a tunnel on its side, and the bright sky is so far above her head. The rocks are not rocks, but bones, and the bones come together until an army of tiny, toothless skeletons surround her.

There are too many to fight, and they seem so small and helpless, she can't possibly hurt them. She won't. But they outnumber her, and they overtake her. Leaping onto her and pawing at her with their stubby little digits, poking at her eyes and her mouth. Pushing into her ears and her nostrils. She dare not scream. She looks up to the sky, hoping to see her rescuer, but instead she sees herself. Sara Bissett is staring down from the sky, watching herself be taken by the marked ones. The chosen ones. The daughters of Demeter.

There is someone behind her, someone else standing behind Sara. Stephanie. Stephanie will help her. Stephanie understands what is happening. She reaches up with her left hand, her marked hand, pleading in silence for help. Instead, Stephanie pushes Sara into the well, and now she is falling onto herself. She is falling but Sara changes as she falls. Sara of the bones watches as Sara of the fall changes, her hair falls away, her skin becomes translucent, her body almost gelatinous as hands and feet widen into flippers. As she falls toward herself, aquatic Sara opens her mouth, needle-like teeth shining with toxic spittle, and she screams a banshee scream. Sara of the baby bones sits up in bed and screams, too.

"Hey now. It's okay. You're okay." Roy gave her shoulders a little shake to fully wake her.

"There were twins, weren't there? Twins and one had a birthmark, right?"

"Never saw no twins."

"Damnit, Roy, enough. Merry was pregnant. You left that part out, but it's true. She was pregnant when you knew her."

"Suppose I may have kept some things to myself."

"Did she have twins?"

"I told you, I never seen any twins."

Sara's head added an exclamation to every word spoken, her throat hurt from screaming, and every movement brought pain. She shut her eyes.

"Merry delivered around the time of my birthday, and I feel like there is some kind of connection there."

"Makes sense you'd feel that way, bein' here and all."

"You took all those pictures. Did you leave the ledger for me? Why?"

"I took a lot of photos in my younger days. Fancied myself a photographer, but I quit all that after the clan disappeared. Didn't have it in me anymore."

"But you gave them to me. Why?"

"Figured maybe it'd help you with your project."

"But you wanted me to leave here, wanted me out."

"Sooner you finished your book, the quicker you'd leave."

"But what does the ledger mean? What are the numbers?"

"Don't know. Found it in the house after they disappeared. Thought you might make sense of it."

It was too much, too much to consider in her state. Her head throbbed; the room rocked as if she was still within the waters of her dream. Nausea roiled in her guts until her salivary glands responded with a mouthful of spit and her jaw quivered. "Oh God, move!"

She shoved past him and ran to the bathroom. The first heave brought up a mouthful of bitter bile that she managed to hold onto until she reached the toilet.

"Aaahh," she moaned as another spasm hit and the toilet water changed from clear to brownish green. Her head shrieked in protest, as an invisible ice pick jabbed into her eyes with each purge.

Roy was there, a glass of apple juice in his hand. "Here, have a sip. Small one."

She obliged. The sweetness was a welcome balance to the bitterness coating her mouth.

"Your friend stopped by, that Stephanie. She left you a picture. Said you'd been asking for it. Told her you were out of sorts. She came back a little later, brought you some pills. Said she'd talked to the doctor. Got one for the sick and one for sleep. Thinkin' maybe you ought to take one of each."

Sara's guts returned the juice. She wanted to see that picture, to look for twins, but she had an idea she wouldn't see any. Not that there weren't twins being born in the clan, but that only one of the two would survive. She shivered. Could they have sacrificed their own babies? The idea made her heave again, but there was nothing left.

"Here, this one dissolves. Stick it under your tongue."

Sara obliged like a child. Opening her mouth, she lifted her tongue and let Roy drop the pill beneath it.

"Come on, let's head back to bed. I'll bring you a bucket."

She followed him, holding on to his arm to keep her balance. The floor was wobbly. The pill dissolved quickly and left a chalky, cherry taste in her mouth. She wanted another drink of juice. Once in bed, he handed her the glass, along with a second pill.

"I want to see the picture she brought. Did she say anything else?"

"When you wake up, we'll have a look at everything, but for now, you need to sleep."

"What did she say? Did she say anything about the picture?"

"No, she don't say much about the clan, and even if she did, she wouldn't say it to me. Suppose I can understand that."

"I don't understand anything," Sara said and then sleep took her again.

Chapter 31

Sara awoke in the cavern beneath the well, lying atop a pile of fifty-year-old skeletal remains. Babies, all marked for slaughter in the same way she was—an innocuous hemangioma. How had she gotten back down there? Boxes of her favorite snacks were piled along the far wall, Phil's urn sat beside them. It was her home now; she belonged there. Perhaps she'd never left.

Her head no longer ached, and her stomach lay quietly within her, calm as a dead lake. The tunnels were lit as if she wore night vision goggles. In fact, everything was easy to see down there. She reached up to feel the glasses on her face, but there were none. Instead, she felt the rough wrinkles of skin around her eyes, the loss of a distinct nose, and long, thin teeth curving out over her lower lip and down onto her chin.

She opened her mouth to call for help, but she could only produce a small screech reminiscent of the mole-person who had scattered the others away.

No. This can't be real. She'd just been in bed—she was fine, normal. Just a little beat up. She was absolutely not a mole-person. She was marked, yes. Okay, that was true, but if anything, she should be with the babies, the skeletons, one of the daughters of Demeter, not one of these aberrations of nature.

She had to get out of there. Away, back to her room, her bed. If she could do that, everything would go back to the way it was. She would wake up and realize it had all been a bad dream brought on by her grief over the loss of Phil. Andrea was right. Sara Bissett lost her mind and had had no business coming there alone.

She knew which tunnel would take her back to the house. She knew them all as if they were hallways in her home and could easily see within them. With mole skin and claws, she flew through the tunnel without difficulty. She could smell where grubs lay just under the surface and knew a plump beetle lumbered across the trail ahead. Her stomach lurched toward it, and it took all of Sara's will not to snatch it up and crunch it between her powerful teeth.

The tunnel spilled into the root cellar of the Demeter house. On four feet, she continued across the dirt floor and up the soft wooden stairs to the kitchen. The corner door was unlocked, so she let herself in and passed into the living room, where she hesitated only slightly to glance at a painting of her likeness standing near the orchard.

Have to get to bed, back to bed and sleep, then I'll wake up and everything will be normal again.

As she crawled up the steps, something inside her squirmed. Movement from within made her nauseous, so instead of to the bed, she went to the bathroom. Pulling herself up, she threw up again in the toilet, only this time it was not green bile. It was dirt and grubs and bugs of various sizes. They squirmed and wallowed among the vomitus. Horrified, she crawled up the sink and turned on the cold water, splashing it into her face over and over.

When she finally looked in the mirror, it was not Sara Bissett's reflection but a mole's—no, the *behemoth* mole's—staring back at her. Those eyes, with their blue-grey hue and pity, looked into her own.

"No!" She sat up in bed. Roy jumped from his slumber in the chair he'd dragged next to her.

"Have you seen the monsters?" she asked.

"No."

"No? Aren't you going to ask me 'what monsters?' or 'what are you talking about?'"

"Don't need to. I know what you're referrin' to."

"Because you've seen them. You have to have seen them. Living here all these years. I've been here for a few weeks and I've seen them all! One even attacked me." She pulled the covers off her legs, showing him the gashes. "The lake monster did this! I had its skin under my nails. I sent it to my friends at U of M for analysis."

Roy touched her hand and pulled the blanket back over her. "No need to get yourself all worked up. This place has a way of messin' with people's heads."

"Bullshit. You're just trying to make me think I'm crazy. I'm not crazy, and you know it, Roy. I know you know it. I know you've seen them, too. I know it."

"Never seen any twins, never seen any monsters of any sort. Heard plenty of crazy stories about this place. Seen it do some crazy things to people. Look what it's doin' to you."

"This is insane. When that DNA test comes back, my friends will come. I'll show them the caves and the tunnels. Bill will dive the lake. Then everyone will see."

"No one ought to be coming here until you're better and you're thinkin' straight again. You'll scare all them college kids with this kind of talk."

"Get out of my house. Get out!" She hit at him, pushing him off the chair. "Get out! I never want to see you again."

Roy put his hands up in surrender. "Okay, okay. I'll go, but I think you should, too. As soon as possible. Will you do that for me?"

"No." She closed her eyes and turned her head away. She didn't look again until after she heard the front door close gently and Roy's steps fade away down the porch stairs.

Chapter 32

Two days had passed since she'd kicked Roy out. Two days of headaches and vomiting, but no more dreams, and Sara considered that to be a win. On the third morning, after she'd vomited up the little bit of grilled cheese she'd managed to eat the day before, she actually felt hungry. Miraculously, her headache was gone, her energy was back, and for the first time in a long time, she felt like herself.

There could be no more putting off the voicemails from Andrea. There were three but at least ten missed calls. She opened the oldest of the messages.

"Sara, it's Andrea. Bill got the reports back on the tissue sample you sent him. He wasn't sure how to tell you, so I offered to do it for him. It's all your DNA. Sara, do you understand? Both your blood sample and the tissue sample match. There is no lake monster, there are no monsters. It's all your mind fucking with you. You need counseling and you need to get out of that house. You can call Bill if you have any questions. Bye."

"Bullshit. I will call Bill because I don't believe you, Andrea. You're just being spiteful." Sara saved it and moved on to the next message.

"Hey, so Bill and I have been talking. We decided that you are in no state to have students up there and as it seems you insist on staying, we've had no choice but to cancel the class. No one is coming up, Sara. Not me, not Bill. It's become clear to all of us that the town and their long-held beliefs coupled with some strange people feeding you crazy stories has led to your already stressed mind completely cracking. Get help, Sara."

"Arrgghh," Sara grunted and threw the phone down. She didn't want to hear any more of what Andrea had to say. Instead, she would spend her uninterrupted time here at Demeter house solving the mystery. That included proving the existence of the creatures living there with her.

No one else can help because I am connected to this place, and I'm the only one who's seen all its secrets. I'm the only one with a chance of solving it.

164

"You might even say my DNA is here, right, Andrea?" She snorted a laugh.

On the table in front of her, the recently returned photo lay next to a neat stack of all the other pictures, sitting beside the ledger. A young Stephanie dancing beside the other children of the cult. Why hadn't Stephanie told her about that? Hell, why hadn't Roger told his wife who it was in his childhood picture with him? Could anyone in this town be trusted?

The photos of a lost time consumed her thoughts. She'd memorized every face, every child, every pregnancy, and yet there was something missing. Something she should have realized, but it eluded her.

She opened the ledger and the page of her notes blew off the table onto the floor. Leaning over on the chair, the dog tags slid across her breast. She grabbed the notes and sat up, pulling the tags free from her shirt. Hadn't she left them on the table?

In the light of morning, with clear eyes, she was able to read the soldier's name. *Kumpula, Roy P.*

"Roy," she said out loud. "Of course."

He knew a lot more than he was telling. The time had come, now that she was back in her right mind, for him to tell her everything. She grabbed her phone, intending to record the whole conversation, and slipped on her shoes, three-day-worn sweatpants and tee shirt be damned.

She swung the side door open with full intent and screamed.

Stephanie stopped, wide eyed. Her hand frozen in a protestor's fist about to knock on the door. In her left arm, she cradled a big manila envelope and a brown take-out bag from Slim's. Once their surprised shock wore off, Stephanie moved forward.

"I come bearing gifts. First, soup. I know you're feeling better. Roger told me Roy was back at the farm again. Still, if you ask me, soup is the best medicine, and this—she pulled a quart of soup from the bag—is Slim's cream of chicken with noodles. Don't even try to say no.

While the smell, to most, might be delicious, for Sara it triggered her gag reflex. Swallowing it back, she opened the door further and stepped aside.

"Come on in. I've missed you. I'm feeling a lot better actually."

"Yeah, Roy told Rog you took a fall and got a concussion! That's terrible. I don't know if he told you but I stopped by. Brought you some medicine."

"Oh yes. Thank you so much! That nausea med worked great."

"Good. I'm glad. Listen, Sara, I need to come clean about something—"

Sara interrupted. "I know that's you and Roger in the picture. Your grandfather told me. I think I understand why you didn't say at first. I mean, I think I know what's going on with you and Roger."

"Oh. Um, well, that is something I suppose we'll have to talk about soon enough. But no, it's about the podcast. Have you heard it?"

"The one Reggie and Stu did? I was here when they recorded it." Whatever Stephanie was getting at, Sara hadn't a clue. Clearly, the woman thought it was important.

"No, the one they posted yesterday. You didn't know?"

"They did another one about this place?"

"Get some bowls and spoons. We'll eat and listen. I want you to hear it before I show you what's in the envelope."

The Mysterious Creepcast, *episode 2 of The Children of Demeter*

Intro: Welcome to another episode of *The Mysterious Creepcast* where your hosts Reg and Stu are creepin' it real with true tales of strange places. Come on in…if you dare.

Reg: Hey, hey. It's your buds Reggie and Stu back for another trip into the creepy and mysterious world we live in.

Stu: That's right. This shit is the real deal, my friends. We don't play around. Each week, we broadcast live from haunted, cursed, or otherwise fucked up places where all sorts of weird shit happened.

Reg: Today, we're visiting with a previous guest of the show. Roy Kumpula, farmer, neighbor, and previous lover of a member from the Children of Demeter cult. Roy notified us that he had more information he wanted to share, so we've got him on the phone all the way from the Demeter house.

Stu: Welcome back, Roy.

Roy: Thank you, boys.

Reg: Right now, you're at the house taking care of our friend, who is recovering from a bad fall, is that right?

Roy: You remember helping her get that cover off the old well? She went out the other night in the dark, forgot about it being opened, and took a tumble. I heard her and found her right away. She'll be okay after some rest, is all.

Reg: So glad you were there. I know she's going through a rough time; we all feel better knowing she has you looking after her.

Stu: You said you wanted to clarify a few things and asked if we could have you back on the show. When we last spoke, you'd told us that the girl you fell for, Merry, sort of ghosted you after the sex in the cave. She refused to see you or speak to you. A year later, the whole clan was gone.

Roy: Yeah, I said that, but it ain't the truth. Not the whole truth, anyway. Sitting here, watching over your friend, Sara, got me thinking it was time to tell the story the way it happened. Repercussions, be damned.

Reg: What you told us before, none of that was true?

Roy: Most of it was true. I just left out a big chunk of the middle.

Stu: Well, you're back now, Roy. It's never too late.

Roy: I hope you're right, son. I truly do.

Reg: So, why don't you tell us where we need to pick the story back up? Where does the part you left out begin?

Roy: You know the part when I said I confronted her in the house, and she wouldn't talk to me? By then, we'd actually had a few conversations.

Stu: You did see her and speak to her after your steamy cave sex?

Roy: Oh yeah. Things between us were about the same. Not that I wanted it that way, but she did. I'd visit, and we'd talk, just like before. Met up many a time in the greenhouse where she did her chores. Within a few months, I could see she was pregnant.

Stu: WHAT? You got Merry pregnant?

Roy: I asked her a few times if the baby was mine. She said, "No baby belongs to you or me or any of us. We, and they, are the children of Demeter."

Reg: But didn't you think it had to be yours? I mean, come on, right?

Roy: At the time, I didn't know. I wasn't sure then that I wanted it to be mine. I mean, what did I know about kids? And you asked about orgies and such—there were. Mostly involving Rolf, er, Esmond. So, it seemed to

167

me he'd probably fathered most of the kids running around up there. Now, looking back on it—yeah, that baby was mine.

Reg: My man, I'm sorry.

Roy: Oh, we went back and forth on it as she kept getting bigger. All the pregnant girls up here got big like that. Almost like they grew their babies like they did their fruits and vegetables. Big and healthy. Merry kept getting bigger, and the bigger she got, the harder I pushed. We argued, I threatened, and then she withdrew. That was the day I went to the house, walked in, and demanded to see her.

Stu: Did you get to see her?

Roy: No. It was just like I said. She refused to see me. Said she never wanted to see me again. All that was true. I saw the mural, but there were no monsters on it. Those came much later, like years after they disappeared.

Reg: Wait, so, someone else came, after the others disappeared and painted the monster into the mural?

Roy: Guess Sara hasn't given you an update. There're three monsters painted on this wall. All different. One by the water, one by the caves and one near a tunnel by the orchard.

Stu: You're shittin' me! Reg, we gotta get out there, do an update.

Reg: Yeah, well, let's let Roy finish, and let my auntie get better, then we'll talk.

Stu: Yeah, you're right. So, Roy, did you ever see or talk to her again? I mean, what about her baby? Did they disappear before she had it or what, man?

Roy: Yep, I saw her. Middle of the night, it was pouring rain. She's pounding on the door. 'Course I didn't know it was her til I opened it, and saw Merry soaked to the bone, hunched over a squalling newborn. She was hysterical. Merry, I mean, not the baby—she was also a girl. I pulled her inside, out of the rain. "She's marked. I can't let them take her," she said. She showed me a fan-shaped birthmark on the baby's left hand. "You have to get her away from here. Far away. Tonight. Promise me you will?" I took the babe. I asked her, "Who is trying to take her from you?" I tried to understand her, but she was a ravin' lunatic. "The cult, the Goddess. She's marked!" She showed me the baby's hand again. The little thing quieted, then. Wrapped her little hand around my thumb. "Merry," I said. "I have to know if she is mine."

Reg: She refused to tell you? Even then?

Roy: She just shook her head. "It doesn't matter," she said. "You can't keep her. Not here, not this close to the house or the fields. She'll never be safe here. The Goddess wants her." Like I said, she was raving. "Just take her away, tonight. As far as you can and find her a good home. Please, Roy, if you ever loved me, do this. There's no time. The ceremony is set for tomorrow. Take her now, please."

Stu: She gave you the baby? Woo, man, what did you do?

Roy: I looked at that precious bundle, and I saw my features, my family in her face, in her lips, her pout. I knew in my heart she was my daughter, but I also believed Merry, that she wasn't safe. So, I knew I would do as her mother asked. "On one condition," I told Merry. "When I get back, I want you to tell me everything. What is going on here?" She nodded, tears still running down her cheeks, but she'd stopped with the hysterics. "I will," she said. "Everything, I promise." She kept nodding. She handed me a bag with bottles, and, I suppose, breastmilk. "This is enough for two days. Take her as far as the milk supply lasts, feed her every two to three hours." Then she ran off. Just opened the door and ran back into the rain. It was the last time I seen her.

Stu: Do you think, when she'd promised she'd tell you everything, that she knew she would never see you again? Do you think they killed her?

Roy: I suspect she knew she might never see me again. I'm not sure they killed her, seein' as how none of them were around when I got back. They'd all disappeared.

Reg: So, what did you do with the baby?

Roy: I left that night, drove as far as I could until I was falling asleep. Me and the little missus, we stayed the night in a cheap motel. She kept me up for a while, not wanting to settle down without her mom, and I ended up oversleeping the checkout. Had to pay for another day. So, we stayed, napping off and on all day until nightfall, when I finally felt rested. We got back on the road. Made it all the way to Fort Wayne, Indiana, before the milk supply ran out. It was a sunny day, so I walked her around a park for a while, just enjoying her presence. Told her about myself and my family, hoping foolishly that she'd remember me and maybe come find me someday.

Stu: Maybe she will, man. Maybe she will.

Roy: Possible. So, I took her to the local shopping mall, and we did some people watching. I saw a nice-looking couple sharing French fries on a bench. I set the babe on the bench beside the young lady while they were doing some smoochin' and I walked away. I kept an eye on them, making sure they noticed her. But Little Miss wasn't one to be seen and not heard. She made sure they found her. Once she was in the woman's arms, I left.

Reg: Goddamn, that must have been tough. So sorry, my man.

Roy: Yep, hardest thing I've ever had to do...til now, I suppose. Telling you fellas, confessin' my sins, might be a wee bit tougher. She ever listens to this or figures it out, I suppose she'll hate me.

Stu: Nah, man, you saved her. She'll understand that.

Reg: So, when you got home, the place was abandoned?

Roy: Yep. Demeter house was empty, as if they'd all just up and disappeared. All their stuff was there but none of them. The truck was there. I tried to go out and look in the caves, but the land had turned to swamp in two days' time.

Stu: That's nuts.

Roy: Yep. Wasn't long after that when things started dying off. The land just up and quit. Merry and me used to feed the fish in the pond, sometimes ducks, too. I went up there a couple weeks after I got over the shock—the water was dead. Nothing—and I mean *nothing*—was in it. Not even bugs or frogs.

Reg: How long after the disappearance did you discover the monsters drawn on the mural?

Roy: Oh, probably couple years later? Place was a local haunted attraction for kids. Shooed them away all the time. One little girl came up from time to time. Most days, she'd just sit by the pond. Sometimes I'd see her go in the house. Once in a while, she'd have a little boy with her.

Stu: Why'd you let them stay?

170

Roy: Well, don't know that I can say. Suppose that's their story to tell, if they choose to. But I felt like she had a right to be there, maybe more so than me. Been thinkin' maybe 'twere she painted those monsters. 'Course I don't know that for certain.

Reg: You know, we'd love to talk to her, too, Roy. If you ever run into her or know how to get a hold of her, maybe you can pass our info along?

Roy: Suppose I could. Doubt she'll want to talk. She sure don't like me none, either. But I will when I see her again.

Reg: Great. So that's quite the tale, Roy. Is there anything else you want to add?

Roy: Guess, I'd just say there's a lot in this world that you can't explain. And sometimes the best thing to do is to look the other way. The more you try to figure it out, the more dangerous it becomes. You know the saying "let sleeping dogs lie?" That's what I'm suggesting to you.

Stu: If that's how you feel, what made you decide to tell us the rest of the story? Why didn't you let it lie?

Roy: I suspect whatever was lying, woke up and so, I thought I better tell the whole thing 'fore it's too late.

Stu: Well, if that's not the perfectly freaky ending, I don't know what is. Thanks again for coming on the show, Roy. And, folks, we'll keep you updated if anything more comes of the Children of Demeter story.

Outro: Come find us next week where all things are lost and everything's creepy. Until then, Reg and Stu are ghosts.

Chapter 33

Sara stared at Stephanie's phone long after the podcast ended. She hadn't touched the soup which was now cold. Stephanie reached out and grabbed Sara's hand, giving it a squeeze.

"Are you okay?"

"I was left, as a baby, at a mall in Fort Wayne. My adopted parents were related to the couple that found me." Sara looked up at Stephanie, searching her eyes for empathy or treachery, she wasn't sure what. "Roy and Merry…and me." Sara scratched at her birth mark. "I was that baby?"

"I wasn't sure. I mean, I didn't know *all* the details about your adoption except what you told me about being abandoned at a mall, that and I couldn't help but notice how much you looked like Merry. When I told Roger, well…he found these at Roy's place and I think you better have a look." Stephanie pushed the envelope toward her. Sara put her hand on it but did not take it or open it. There was so much to evaluate here. So much to process. Could she possibly take any more information in right now?

"Roger *found* these?" She asked Stephanie. Stephanie shrugged.

"I guess. That's what he said. He showed them to me and we decided that you needed to see them."

Roger found them in Roy's house when Roy was here. Roger was so helpful and yet, always seemed to stand in her way. Why was he going through Roy's things?

"Are you going to look at them?" Stephanie asked, urging her on.

Sara pulled a stack of photos and newspaper clippings out of the envelope and laid them on the table in front of her like a tarot card spread.

The newspaper clippings were from a Fort Wayne paper and one from Ann Arbor. They followed the plight of Baby M (for mall—*how original*) from being found on a bench to her forever home in Ann Arbor. There was even a follow up piece done on the child's fifth birthday, although her name and parents' names were not released.

And then there were the pictures of the baby taken by someone, most likely Roy. Baby M-to-be lying on a bed, on the seat of a truck, on a differnt bed, taking a bottle. There was one, however, that drew her attention more than the others. In it, the baby held onto a man's thumb with her left hand. On the webbing of that hand, a fan-shaped birthmark darkened her skin—in the exact same shape and location as Sara's.

"Oh God. This is me."

"Of course it's you, Sara. All of this is about you." Stephanie swept her arm encompassing everything around them. "All of this is *because* of you."

"But where did Roger find these pictures? Why wouldn't Roy give them to me before?"

Ignoring the Roger question, Stephanie said, "Who knows why that man does anything he does?" Stephanie's lips thinned and her temple pulsed as she clenched her jaws. Sara had never seen her like this.

"Roy took all these pictures after he kidnapped you and damned the whole commune to a fate worse than Hell. See that quilt you're lying on in this one? His mother made it; Roger says he still uses it, in fact."

An unease rolled up her neck and its prickly fingers massaged her scalp. Stephanie hated Roy because she blamed Roy for what happened to the clan, and what happened to the clan was due to the absence of Sara. And Roger…what role did the elusive Roger play in all of this? She needed a minute to process.

"I'm going to go grab a bottle or two of mead. You up for a glass? I know I need some to help deal with all of this." Sara asked.

"Sure, that sounds great." For a woman who smiled as much and as naturally as she did every day, she should know better than to try to fake one. Yet she did and Sara caught it.

"I'll be right back."

The cellar air was cool and fresh like petrichor. Sara stopped at the bottom of the stairs, leaned her head back, and closed her eyes. Deep breaths in through the nose, out through the mouth, like every good article on anxiety recommended.

Once she'd slowed her racing thoughts and had them lined up for one-at-a-time consideration, she opened her eyes. Standing directly in front of her, about six feet away, the giant mole-person from before stared, motionless.

"Oh God." Sara drew a sharp intake of air, throwing off her cultivated, rhythmic breathing.

The creature did not move, but her eyes locked on Sara's and pleaded with her wordlessly. There seemed to be so much humanity, empathy, maybe even love in those eyes, Sara couldn't break her gaze.

The thing stepped back once, twice, a third time slowly and deliberately ensuring Sara followed. Sara did as the creature's eyes begged her to do, following the thing all the way to the burrow in the wall. Forgetting Stephanie waiting upstairs, she climbed into the tunnel system once again, and joined the colony of monsters that "didn't exist."

She didn't have her phone but didn't need the light anyway; the scuttle of the mole-person maneuvering through was enough to guide her. She assumed they'd stop in the center hub where the other mole people and the baby skulls tried to kill her last time, but instead they took a branch veering away from the center. Imagining the layout in her head, she thought they might be heading toward her car beyond the stone archway but she wasn't sure.

As the tunnel widened and sloped upward, the top of the greenhouse came into view.

"Why are we here?" Sara asked, not expecting an answer. There was an answer though, not from the creature, who crawled out of the tunnel to allow Sara room to emerge before retreating back to safety underground. The answer came from the shouting and choking noises just outside the greenhouse.

Sara peeked around the entryway to see Roy, tangled in the full, lush vines bordering their respective yards, and Roger…and a rifle.

She stepped out and yelled "Hey!" before she'd thought it through. She had no plan really and had no idea what their plans were.

They both looked at her, and that's when she noticed the greenery wrapped tightly around Roy's neck, strangling him.

"Run, Sara!" he choked out. She ignored his command and ran closer. Roger picked the rifle up off the ground and pointed it at her.

"Back off, girl," He warned. She stopped and put her hands up.

"Woah, Roger. I don't know what's happening here but I'm no threat to you. We need to help Roy."

"I don't think so. No. He can die. I'm tired of slaving away on this piece of shit farm and getting nothing in return. And you can die too." He cocked the gun.

"Roger no! Not like that," Stephanie yelled from the front porch.

Sara's gut tumbled to her feet. *Stephanie too?*

Roy's face was swelling. Sara had once seen a photo of dead bodies from the Jonestown suicides and the article described the purple color as "livor mortis"—meaning the blood had pooled into the parts of the body that lay closest to the ground via gravity. Roy's livor mortis defied gravity because the tight botanical noose kept the blood from going to his feet. He was going to die. His brain was deprived of oxygen and that was no good for life sustaining neural activity.

"Run away, get away. I'm sorry, Sara," Roy managed before he passed out. She was going to save him the way he once saved her. Fuck Roger and his gun.

She turned as if to run away and caught a glimpse of Stephanie coming down the steps before she switched directions abruptly and lunged at Roger and the gun. She caught him by surprise and managed to knock the rifle from him. It fell at her feet. She made the grave mistake of looking down at it, allowing Roger to grab her by the hair on the back of her head and yank.

She kicked him in the crotch. He let go.

Sara grabbed the gun and pulled the trigger before she could stop herself. Roger fell in a spray of blood. She dropped the gun, hands shaking, legs jelly, but managed somehow to get to Roy. She knew, behind her, Stephanie was coming. She knew she should grab the gun. There was simply no time for any of that. Right then, she had to save Roy.

She tore at the vines, but as soon as she got one pulled away, another wrapped itself tightly around him. Roger groaned. He wasn't dead, at least not yet.

"I'm so sorry," she sobbed to Roy. She didn't want to have to touch the gun, not ever again, but she couldn't just leave it there for Stephanie or, God-forbid, Roger to use. She pitched it overhand into the field behind Roy, and then she ran.

She didn't dare to go back to the greenhouse. That would mean passing Roger, and she'd seen plenty enough horror movies to know the villain always gets back up after the first shot. She didn't want him grabbing her ankle, or worse yet, following her into the tunnel for a claustrophobic death. She also couldn't go to the car or call for help. The keys and her phone were inside and Stephanie stood between her and the house. Her best shot at escape was the cave. From there she could go back into the tunnels and lose any followers among the many branching tunnels. Also, the chance of finding the one friendly mole-person to protect her would be greater that way.

With focus on the poppy field, she ran past Stephanie, certain she was faster.

"Sara! Wait! Sara, I just want you to understand. Please." Stephanie fell into a jog behind her, but Sara reached the field easily before her.

She rolled her ankle on the unexpectedly soft ground and the next step sunk deeper into the mire. The instability offered no support to her aching ankle. Sara put her arms out like a tight-rope walker trying to maintain balance. She stole a glance over her shoulder. Stephanie had caught up and was stepping into the mire with her. Only, when Stephanie's foot landed, the ground was somehow solid again. She easily traversed the distance.

"Sara, please. You have to understand. This is so much bigger than you or me. No matter what, we have to fix this."

This was madness. She could not take the time to respond. Pulling her legs up one by one, she took long, exaggerated strides. Every step, the earth was looser and wetter than the last. Yet, only for her. Stephanie was doing just fine.

"This all happened because Roy took you away, kept you from your destiny. Only we can fix it. You and me, Sara. We have to make things right. It might just save your mom and your sister and my mom too. Don't you want that?"

Her sister? She knew nothing about having a sister. There were no other babies in the pictures, no one else mentioned a twin in the clippings. Her breathing was ragged and roared in her ears; her chest heaved with effort. The muscles in her legs burned, begging her to stop. The caves were at least a football field away yet. She couldn't stop.

The changing conditions in the poppy swamp kept Stephanie at a consistent distance as long as she kept moving. But she so wanted to stop and ask questions. Did Stephanie have a gun too? If she stopped, what would happen?

I'll stop when I get to the cave.

EV Knight

She would use that mantra to keep going. Stop at the cave, ask the questions, and escape as needed into the underground. Leeches clung to her bare legs; she seemed to pick up more hangers-on with every plunge into the mire.

My sister? A sister? A twin? I'm a twin, but Merry only gave one baby to Roy. Where did the other one go?

A stab of pain drilled into the web of flesh between her thumb and forefinger as if someone jabbed a needle into a voodoo doll of Sara, right in the center of her birth mark.

"Ouch!" she yipped and scratched the mark. The new, healing flesh sent signals to her brain begging for her to stop.

"Sara! Just let me talk to you. I'm your friend. I really am. I care about you and if you listen, I know you'll agree with what we have to do."

She lost her shoes at the halfway point. The gritty yet slimy substrate oozed between her toes with the occasional sensation that she'd stepped on some small wetlands creature. She couldn't think about it. She refused to see the engorged, black invertebrates sucking away at her shins. Stems of underwater plants cut into her skin in their attempt to slow her down but she felt nothing. Numb from the knees down, except for the nagging ache in her ankle and the stress-itch of her birthmark, Sara pushed through.

Stephanie's thudded steps on the firmament behind her kept her moving. While her muscles and lungs ached, Stephanie hadn't even increased her respiratory rate.

Just get to the cave. Then get some answers.

But what about Stephanie?

Be prepared to do whatever you have to do to stay alive. I think she wants to sacrifice you.

As if reading Sara's mind, Stephanie said, "You were chosen to be a daughter of Demeter. Imagine if you had been given to her properly? None of the pain you've had to live through would've happened. You'd be in paradise, the daughter of a Goddess."

"There is no Goddess, Stephanie! Listen to yourself!" She stopped long enough to scream before wading through with every last bit of energy she had.

"Don't say that, Sara. Not right now."

Pain seared up Sara's arm from her birthmark. It was as if she was being branded. The mark bubbled and blistered. The intensity was too much. Her knees buckled and she went down. The cool swamp water should have been soothing but instead, it warmed against her skin until it was the temp of a hot bath, further burning her already ruined flesh.

"Oh Sara, I tried to tell you." Stephanie walked right up to her. Beside the mire Sara had sunk into, the rest of the ground was solid. The hot tub Sara sat in began to thicken as well but the pain left her incapacitated. Stephanie hooked her forearms under Sara's shoulders and hoisted her out of the muck.

"Ow, ow, ow," Sara sobbed.

"It's gonna be okay. Let's get you to the cave and the pain will stop soon enough."

There was no point in protesting, neither vocally nor physically. Her primitive brain had control now, and her only thoughts were related to the pain. Just as they reached the cave, Sara passed out in Stephanie's strong arms and the pain, as promised, stopped.

Chapter 34

A tickle on her face woke Sara. Her arms and shoulders ached but when she attempted to stretch them, they were pinned behind her back. Emerging further from the black out, she realized her arms were tied behind her back and the tie was attached to her ankles, which forced her knees to bend into a ninety-degree angle. Stephanie sat on her knees in front of Sara with a clay bowl in hand, painting marks on Sara's face and chest.

"Oh good, you're awake. I'm going to set you up onto your knees. It will make painting these symbols on you a lot easier. These symbols are important to the ritual. They call to Demeter and the mutations your absence created. When I make it right, when I give you back to Demeter, I pray that she sees fit to return my mother and the rest of my clan family to their proper bodies."

"You painted those monsters on the mural! And you gave them symbols, didn't you?" Sara accused. She had to do something, to keep Stephanie talking until she could work at the ties binding her hands. They didn't feel all that tight and were some sort of plastic rather than rope.

Stephanie set the bowl down. Ignoring Sara's accusations, she got up to tighten the knots keeping Sara on her knees.

"Roger was supposed to do this part. He had the zip ties, but you surprised us both with that shot. I had to improvise." She laughed. "If you could see this you'd laugh. I have you tied up with pennant flags I had in my purse. A realtor's must have for open houses! I've never tried them for this sort of thing, so please be gentle with them."

The candles on the altar were lit, throwing flickering shadows on Sara's baby pictures, which had been lined up on the edge of the flat rock. On the ground, in front of the tableau, was one of Sara's kitchen knives—the big chef's knife.

Stephanie came around to finish her task and followed Sara's eyes.

"Oh, yeah, the knife. Sorry about that too. Again, Roger was supposed to bring the sickle from Roy's farm. It seemed perfectly fitting for the whole thing, but well, you know what happened. So, I grabbed one from your kitchen. Even after what you did to Roger, I'm really sorry, Sara. I understand why you hurt him and, in another life, I'm sure you and I would have been good friends for the rest of our lives. I wish you weren't the lost baby, I didn't want it to be you."

"Whatever this is about, we can work it out, Stephanie. I'm a sociologist, remember? I really do understand the group mentality. I understand you still feel drawn to this place, to the family you lost. I want to help. I just need to understand what you think my role is in this." Sara pleaded.

"I think you know by now, Sara. You were the marked twin. You still have the mark. You were supposed to be sacrificed to Demeter. She *chose* you. But then your mother and Roy sinned against her. Every other mother in the clan understood there would need to be sacrifices. And Demeter, having had her own child taken from her, understood how much she was asking, so she always gave our mothers two babies—one to keep, and one to give away. You see? You were never meant to live here. You were meant to live in paradise with Demeter. Why wouldn't you want that?"

"What kind of God or Goddess turns their followers into monsters? Why would you want to worship her? Why do this after you see what she can do?"

"Those *monsters* are our mothers, and your sister, and our family, Sara! That is the punishment Demeter determined appropriate for letting you get away. Don't you see? We have to make this right. Your sister shouldn't be suffering alone in that lake. Your mother wallowing in the dirt, my mother hiding and withering away in the darkness of this cave."

"Stephanie, you escaped, too. You escaped the punishment. What if you do this then Demeter decides to punish you? Have you considered that?"

"When I give Demeter her daughter back, the daughter who was lost for forty-six years, I know she will reward me by giving my family back to me. It has to be true, Sara. That's why I have to do this. I'm so sorry. I really do consider you my friend, but we have to do the right thing." She put the bowl aside and picked up the knife.

"It's not like I haven't suffered. I lost Roger and now, he's hurt. You hurt him real bad, Sara. I don't know how we'll explain that away. Maybe we can blame it on Roy? He's dead now, so it won't hurt him." She stopped for a moment,

180

seemingly considering that story playing out. "But everyone knew that old fool liked Roger. Plus, that would probably put into question the validity of the will leaving it all to Rog. No, we can't do that. We're going to have to blame it on you. I hate to add insult to injury, but it'll have to be done."

"You don't have to do this, Stephanie. Think about it. If Roy is dead," she swallowed hard on the thought. There was so much she'd wanted to say to him. "Then we can say that they came to help with an intruder and were attacked." The ties were loosening up. She worked her hands and feet in little circles, trying to keep Stephanie's attention away from any movement.

"I'm going to try to make this fast for you, Sara. I don't want you to suffer any more. But I need you to hold still. I need you to understand that if we are to undo everything that has happened since you were stolen away, you have to accept your destiny."

"Wait!" Stephanie and Sara looked out the cave entrance. Roger was ambling through the field, his left arm hung and swung limply at his side. He held his left shoulder with his right hand. The grimace on his face and the gritted teeth betrayed the pain he was trying to work against. "I want to be there when you kill the bitch. I want to watch the life go out of her eyes. I got the sickle." Her would-be execution device dangled from his belt.

The candles flickered. There was movement near the tunnels. Were the creatures coming to watch, to celebrate her death, her return to their Goddess?

"No, no Stephanie, please," she sobbed.

She turned her attention to the cave's tunnels, watching, hoping, sending telepathic messages to her mole-person ally—*my mother?*—to save her.

"Roger!" Stephanie gasped and Sara looked back. He was sinking and quickly into the suddenly changing ground. "Roger hurry, get in here!"

But he was gone, just like that. The ground turned to water beneath him and he sunk. One moment his head was there, and the next, it was gone. He was gone.

"No!" Stephanie screamed and ran out to the spot he'd vanished. But the ground was as solid as it had been for her all along. She dug frantically at the ground, but there was no doubt, Demeter had swallowed him up. He was gone.

Sara worked frantically at the pennant ties and almost had her hand loose when Stephanie growled and ran at her. Grabbing the knife up off the ground, she brought it back across her body, ready to sever Sara's head right off. Sara shut her eyes tight and held her breath. At least it would be fast.

But instead, a loud thud, followed by an "oof!" from Stephanie. The clatter of the knife on the ground caused Sara to open her eyes again.

The outcast mole-person, her mother, was on top of Stephanie, clawing at her face and hair. Stephanie squirmed and kicked and covered her face with her hands. Surrounding the two wrestlers, were a group of mutants. Most likely some were Stephanie's family of cave dwellers, and other members of the cult if Stephanie was to be believed.

Sara couldn't waste any time thinking about that. She worked her left hand out of the bind and managed to get ahold of the knife. If she could cut herself free, she could help in the fight. She didn't want to hurt anyone, but after Roger, she knew she could if it came to that. She would not let Stephanie hurt the poor creature, and she would prefer not to sacrifice anyone else to a crazed and angry Goddess.

Cutting the ties behind her back left-handed proved to be more difficult than she suspected. It always looked so easy in the movies. She dropped the knife twice and cut her heel once. She tried to ignore the fight scene in front of her. The grunts from the creature and the cries from Stephanie. The other monsters were slowly closing in, tightening the circle around them. It was like a playground fight, nervous spectators unsure of what role to play, if any.

Stephanie managed to wriggle away just as Sara released the ties. She put her hands up defensively as the woman lunged at her. The mole-person that could, in some strange way, be Sara's biological mother, took no time to leap onto Stephanie's back.

"Get off!" Stephanie yelled through bloodied, swollen lips. She raised up and arched her back just as Sara swung the knife around to defend herself.

But, then, the world exploded, and everything went quiet.

Once the shock wore off and Sara was able to establish that everyone in the party was still alive, she turned around assuming Roger had somehow clawed up out of his grave, but Roger was still entombed. Standing on top of his would-be grave was Andrea, holding Reggie's handgun.

"No, Andrea! Don't shoot them." The earth rumbled but Sara did not so much hear it through the high-pitched roaring in her head, but feel it. Crumbles of dirt fell from the ceiling of the cave.

Andrea looked at Sara, eyes wide, her body still trembling. "What?"

Sara could read her lips so she put her hands up and mouthed back "STOP."

"No, Sara. Look!" Andrea ran into the cave, pointing at Stephanie who was being dragged deeper inside the cavern toward the underground tunnels.

Stephanie's voice reverberated off the cave walls enough that Sara could make out most of what she said. "No! No! Not me, not me. Get her. Not me."

"Don't hurt them. They saved me." Sara pushed Andrea's gun down to the floor. The cave floor undulated beneath them as the walls around them began to implode.

"Then we have to get out of here, now!" Andrea shoved Sara toward the entrance as Sara watched the creatures drag Stephanie deeper inside, back into the womb of the earth.

And then, the cave system collapsed swallowing all the children of Demeter, save one.

Chapter 35

When they found Roy, he was lying on the ground, released from the vines. If it weren't for the red bruising on his neck and arms, it could have been assumed he'd had a heart attack. Andrea performed CPR until the paramedics arrived to collect him. Sara could only stare motionless, paralyzed by fear, confusion, disbelief and with what felt like a toxic level of adrenaline coursing through her veins. When the ambulance left with Roy, they did not turn on the lights or siren and Sara knew exactly what that meant. Roy, her father, was dead.

Andrea managed to coax Sara to the house and made her a strong cup of tea with a little whiskey thrown in for good measure.

"I don't suppose you need this validation, but I drove up here to tell you in person that you aren't crazy. Bill found something weird in the tissue you sent. I wanted to go over it with you, and to apologize for everything," Andrea said. She reached out for Sara's hand and Sara closed the distance. "I need you to tell me everything. I'm on your side, really."

"Roy was my dad," Sara sighed.

"I think you're right. When he called Reggie and they did that last podcast, I had the same suspicion. I was going to demand a DNA test when I came up here today, but I think it won't be too much trouble to get a sample now."

Sara choked back a sob. "I wasn't very nice to him."

"He understood. I'm sure he did."

"And my mother was Merry. I think one of those monsters might have once been my mom, Andrea. Does that sound insane?"

"Yep. Sure does, but after everything you've just told me, and what I saw in that cave, who am I to judge?"

"Do you think my DNA matched the lake monster because she was my twin?"

Andrea huffed a small laugh, "You should ask the biologist that question, but I want to be there when you do."

EV Knight

"So, now what?" Sara asked.

"Well, unless he has a will, you're probably going to inherit all of the farm. As for this place, I think it's imperative that we do some research. But given what I saw today, I think we need to keep it as classified as possible. But I guess that's up to you, because you own Demeter house."

"Do you think any of what Stephanie said could be true? I mean, you saw them, too. Andrea, what happened to those people?"

"Honestly, I don't know, but I'm guessing some kind of toxic chemical. Something that changed DNA rapidly, some sort of cancer or skin disease type of toxin. I think it worked on the plant life, too. But I draw the line at this Demeter shit. She is a remnant of an ancient mythology. She doesn't exist, never has. She was a convenient explanation for what happened here. That's all." Andrea looked into Sara's eyes. Sara felt as if Andrea could read her thoughts, could feel her perfectly manicured nails digging around in her brain. "So, I'm sorry, Persephone, but I think this is a job for science not mythology." She grinned and wiggled Sara's healing left hand.

"You know, I think it's time I moved out of my mom's place," Sara smirked through her tears.

"Oh, I've read some stories about your mom. It turns out she doesn't let her daughters move away all that easily," Andrea warned.

"Yeah, I'm afraid of that."

Epilogue

"Come on, now. We're meeting Auntie for lunch," Sara said to the girls.

"Yay!" Mary said skipping over the puddles in the parking lot of The Kumpula Research Institute.

"Mama, look!" Steffy said. She pointed to the small, curling vine that poked through the blacktop of the parking lot.

Sara's heart skipped a beat. Over the past five years, she'd personally seen to it that every inch of the land owned by the Demeter clan was covered. The house was torn down, the caves filled in, and a deep electrified fence surrounded the research institute she'd donated to the university—with the stipulation that all employees were handpicked and administered by Bill and Andrea.

"Don't touch it, okay, love? It could be poisonous." Of course, it would be Steffy to notice it. Steffy, born identical to her sister, except for the large, rust-colored birthmark on her neck. Thank God it faded, what with kindergarten starting soon. She didn't want Steff to have to deal with the bullying that came with marks like that.

"It's not poison, Mama. It's pretty," Steffy said.

"Well, let's not worry about that now. Let's go see Auntie. You'll have to tell her about the new house, and how excited you are for school!" Sara feigned excitement, trying to change the subject.

"Yay, school!" Mary jumped up and down, her sandy-brown curls catching the light of the sun.

"I bet when we come back out here after lunch, there'll be even more vines to see!" Steffy said.

"No there won't, Steffy. You don't know anything."

"That's enough," Sara said. "Let's go."

"I do too know," Steffy muttered. "Demeter told me."

About the Author

EV Knight is the author of the 2020 Bram Stoker Award winning debut novel *The Fourth Whore*. She has also written a novella titled *Dead Eyes* for Unnerving Press's Rewind or Die series. Her short stories and poetry appear in a number of anthologies, magazines, and the HWA's 2019 Poetry Showcase. She received her MFA in Writing Creative Fiction from Seton Hill University in 2019. EV can be found wandering the haunted streets of Savannah, Georgia with her husband Matt, and their four naughty sphynx cats—Feenix, Luna, Bizzabout Fitchett, and Ozymandias Fuzzfoot the First.